This book is loving dedicated to Sharon and Andrew Lewis, and your perfect little girls. Life holds plenty of ups and downs, but never forget that God holds it all in His hands. Let trust and faith guide your every decision.

"A man's heart plans his ways, but the lord directs his steps"
Proverbs 16:9

HOLLY

CRAFTED WITH LOVE, BOOK TWO

SHARON SROCK

A BLONDE AND A PRAYER BOOKS

CHAPTER ONE

Holly Hoffman parked at the curb and swallowed the final bite of her soggy, drive-through burger. Her gaze scanned the items stacked haphazardly on the garage sale's randomly placed tables while she sucked on the straw in her cup. When empty bubbles gurgled from the depths, she put the cup in the holder and reached for the door handle. She hated these sales. They reminded her too much of the hand-me-downs and never-new items of her childhood. But a friend had called with a heads-up about an item she might be able to use, so here she was. And she was just one of many.

Rainy, chillier-than-normal September weather had kept a lot of people inside during the first part of the week. But Friday dawned bright and warm, making it a perfect day to be outside.

She climbed from behind the wheel and slammed the door of her fifteen-year-old Jeep. Sunshine glinted on bare metal scratches in the door, present for longer than she'd owned the vehicle. Holly ignored them with practiced disregard and focused on locating the object of her quest.

One of the tables in the back featured some drooping tinsel and a collection of cheap, boxed Christmas ornaments. That was as good a place to start as any. Her friend had only called thirty minutes before. Hopefully what she'd come for was still here.

Holly picked her way through shoppers and around tables so intent on her goal that she almost missed it. She passed by a table loaded with glassware and discarded knickknacks heading toward the shiny red, green, and gold tinsel.

Holly.

She stopped and turned. A quick study of her fellow shoppers didn't reveal a single person she knew, and no one was looking at her.

So who'd called her name?

Something moved in her peripheral vision, drawing her attention away from the mystery of an unrecognized voice and back to the table stacked with glassware. She retraced her steps and bent to take a closer look. It was the unfinished Nativity set she'd come here to find. A twelve-inch-tall angel stood on the corner of the table, his wings spread, his hands lifted in invitation, his face joyful. The rest of the set surrounded him, packed neatly in open boxes. A cow, a donkey, a shepherd with a lamb around his neck, a kneeling wise man with a jeweled box in his hands, and of course Mary, Joseph, and a baby in a manger.

"Ohh..." Holly picked up the angel, turning him gently in her hands, looking for cracks and chips. She held it up to the light and smiled at the slight translucence of the wings. Next she tested the edge of his robe with a fingernail. The finish was as smooth as an eggshell. He was porcelain, and he was perfect. A quick study of the companion pieces assured her that all of them were in pristine condition. She replaced everything, crossed her arms, and took a step back.

The card next to the set read twenty-five dollars. It wasn't the price that gave her pause. Her business fund had more than enough to cover such a minor expense. No, it wasn't the cost. It was the time involved in taking on such a time-intensive project with a built-in deadline. The set would need to be painted, fired after each round of paint, and finally glazed. It'd need to be on display by Halloween for her best chance to sell it by Christmas.

It was already mid-September, and on top of the commitment she'd made to Ember Abbott to keep Ember's store, Crafted with Love, supplied with hand-crafted Christmas ornaments, Holly was cleaning a dozen houses a week, participating in a dog walking service, as well as slowly building an Avon clientele. Her last three orders had topped the five-hundred-dollar mark, and she was on track to crack the next sales level by December.

She tapped her fingers against her lips. Once the Nativity set was complete, she could sell it for a hefty profit. A profit that would go into her car fund. She gave a quiet snort. *Go into? More like finish.* And once she could ditch her old relic for a dependable vehicle, she could add Uber driving to her résumé. With that goal achieved, her finances would be much more secure.

Something fluttered in the corner of her eye.

What the...

The tiny hairs on the back of her neck rose as she leaned in for a closer look at the statuesque angel. Holly would have sworn that the hands that were now clasped under his chin in an attitude of prayer had been raised to the sky just a few seconds ago. Goosebumps prickled her skin as she retrieved the angel with an unsteady hand and tapped one of his wings with a fingernail. He was as solid as the material he was made from.

Of course he was.

Her breath came out in a nervous huff of laughter.

Girl, you've been working too hard. First you're hearing things and now you're seeing things.

Holly traced the delicate sweep of his wings. She could almost imagine bringing him to life with her stock of porcelain paints. Blue and gold for his robe and sash, white and silver for the wings, maybe a little sparkle along the edges for some added pop. Her eyes lost their focus as she looked at the other pieces. She could see them complete and gracing a mantle with candles burning on either side or nestled in the folds of an ornate tree skirt under a

Christmas tree. Either way, her handiwork would become the centerpiece of someone's Christmas.

Holly didn't buy into all that religious stuff. A virgin giving birth to a God come to save the world. *Really?* She shook her head. Life had taught her to depend on herself, but there were plenty of people who did believe, and one of those people would pay handsomely for what she could create.

A gray-haired woman approached and stood beside her. "What a lovely set."

"It's perfect," Holly whispered, her voice a bit dreamy.

"You're holding that angel like he's an inner tube in a raging sea. Are you a buyer or a looker?" the older woman asked. "I've got a granddaughter looking for a high school art project. This just might fii the bill."

Holly swallowed as her vision of perfection dissolved. Suddenly she saw these gorgeous pieces being ruined by a half-hearted teenager. She bit her lip as the woman reached for the figure of the baby.

"Yes." The word escaped Holly's lips in a near shout.

The old woman's hand halted in mid-reach.

"Yes," Holly repeated in a more measured tone. "Sorry, you caught me daydreaming. I was just about to pack them up and pay for them.

The woman dropped her hand to her side. "No problem. Enjoy your project." She stepped over to look at something on the next table.

Holly gathered up the boxes. She didn't understand the sudden compulsion to take them home, but there was no denying that something about these pieces had gotten under her skin. She gave a small deprecating chuckle. It certainly had nothing to with the nonsensical notion that the angel had waved his wings at her. Twice. Nope, she wasn't going there.

~

THIRTY MINUTES later Holly pulled into a narrow spot in the alley behind Crafted with Love. She'd worked all week on a special item for the store and couldn't wait to see what Ember thought. The set of four ceramic, Christmas-themed mugs were an experiment on Holly's part. One she hoped Ember liked well enough to add to the Christmas display.

And what are you going to do if she does? You just bought a Nativity set that will take every spare minute you have to complete. Holly shrugged the question away. She'd cross that bridge once she got there. Sleep was overrated.

Holly scooped up the box of mugs and let herself in the back door of the store. The small break area was empty, but she could hear more than one voice coming from the showroom. She took the time to fix a cup of coffee from the pot Ember kept hot and fresh on the counter before she ducked through the door to find the shop owner. Ember Abbott, was standing next to the front door with the building owner, Dane Cooper. He watched thoughtfully as Ember made broad motions toward the back wall of the store. The wall Holly now found herself in front of. Ember waved a greeting and motioned Holly to the side.

"Nothing fancy," Ember said to Dane. "But I thought if we came down from the ceiling a couple of feet, we could get in three or four rows of shelving on either side of the door. As it is, it's pretty much wasted space. We might as well put it to use."

Dane tilted his head and studied the area. As one innovator to another, Holly could almost see the creative wheels turning inside the head of the handyman/building owner. With a single nod Dane lowered his gaze to Ember.

"I like it."

Ember clapped her hands and bounced up and down on her toes. "Oh, I hoped you would. I could have put up portable units without bothering you, but this isn't something I'll be rearranging, so stationary will just look better. How soon can you start and how long will it take?"

"Women..." Dane muttered, but there was a smile on his face.

He pulled a worn notebook from his back pocket and flipped through a few pages. "The bad news is that my schedule is pretty full. The good news is that I have a helper for the immediate future, and I haven't put him to work just yet. Some simple shelves would be a perfect place for him to start."

When Ember narrowed her eyes at Dane's statement, Holly bowed her head over her coffee to hide a grin. It was clear that Ember was about to take umbrage at having her new pet project foisted off on an untried underling.

As entertaining as the showdown promised to be, Holly hoped that they came to some sort of agreement soon. She took out her phone and studied her schedule. It was almost one. She had another house to clean, and she'd marked herself available to walk dogs between four and six. Not a lot of wiggle room.

"Dane, I know I sprung my idea on you out of the blue. I appreciate your willingness to accommodate me, but if you don't have the time, I'd rather you said so instead of handing the job off to a newbie. I'd rather wait on the shelves than deal with a lot of extra mess and nonsense generated by—"

Dane stopped Ember with an upraised finger. "Hold that thought." He took his phone off the belt clip at his waist and punched in a few numbers. "You still at the spa?"

Holly tuned out Dane and his one-sided conversation. She needed to talk to Ember, and her negotiations with Dane looked like they might take a while longer. With a quick swipe, she opened the dog walking app and removed her name from this evening's calendar. Being your own boss with a flexible schedule had its perks. With her name off that list, if she got a late start on the Roble house, she'd still have plenty of time to finish before the family arrived home at six-thirty. With her schedule adjusted, she turned her attention back to Ember and Dane only to be sidetracked a second time when the bell over the store's door announced a new visitor.

The man coming through the door was tall, broad-shouldered, with a head full of thick dark hair that just brushed his shoulders.

Any woman with a pulse would have fallen prey to the stranger's high cheekbones and generous mouth, but it was his eyes that stole Holly's breath. They were as dark as his hair and surrounded by lashes thick enough to be the envy of any model who'd ever strutted her stuff on one of New York City's fashion runways.

Holly swallowed and gathered her scattered wits. A Greek god had just wandered in off the street, and he looked a little lost. Someone should see what he needed. With Ember occupied, that left Holly. *Dang the luck.*

She took a step forward and paused with a cringe when she caught a glimpse of herself in the mirror attached to Maggie's jewelry display. A faded T-shirt bearing the logo of her favorite soft drink, frayed blue jeans, and scuffed athletic shoes might have been perfect when she'd left home that morning for a day spent cleaning houses, but the outfit fell considerably short of the mark when it came to the task of greeting this incredibly hunky slice of humanity.

Why, why did he have to pick today to come into the store? Why, why was she the only person available to greet him when she looked like a street orphan straight from a Dickens novel? She blew out a frustrated breath. Why was the earth round, why was the ocean salty, why was snow cold? They just were. None of those things was a conspiracy aimed at her, and neither was this.

She straightened her shoulders and prepared to do her duty but froze when Ember gave a little squeal, rushed to the stranger, and threw herself into his embrace.

"Riley. Welcome home."

Strong muscled arms folded around Ember. "Ms. Monroe."

Holly's eyebrows elevated at the deep rumble of his voice. How was it possible to put so much masculine sex appeal into two words?

"No...wait. Not Monroe." He stepped back. "Mom says you got married a couple of weeks ago. Congratulations."

Ember looked up...way up...and gave a loud, exaggerated sigh.

"Thanks. I got tired of waiting on you to grow up. A woman's gotta do what a woman's gotta do."

Holly moved back behind the counter as Riley's rich male laughter filled the store. Holly's next job, and her need to visit with Ember, suddenly found themselves secondary to being busy and inconspicuous so she could find out what she could about Adonis... er...Riley.

Dane inserted himself back into the conversation. "You done flirting with my help?"

Ember put a hand on the younger man's wrist. "Riley is the help you want to give my project to? Why didn't you say so?"

"You didn't really give me a chance. I take it my son meets with your approval."

Ember offered Dane an *are-you-kidding-me* look.

So Riley was Dane's son. Holly tucked that snippet of info away for later consideration.

"Good," Dane said. "Now that we have that settled, let's do this. Why don't I draw up a couple of designs over the next few days? Once you pick out what you like, Riley can get started." He looked at the younger man. "What do you think time-wise?"

Riley turned to study the wall. "Going by what you said over the phone, shouldn't take more than three or four weeks once I get started." He looked down at Ember. "I'm sorry I can't give you my undivided attention. I'm splitting my time between helping Dad and my new job. Will that work for you?"

"Perfect," Ember said. "And thanks to you both." She made dismissive shooing motions with her hands. "Now you two get out of here. The quicker you bring me ideas, the quicker we can get started."

Holly watched them go, heads together, already talking about pine versus oak...the benefits of straight edges versus the appeal of a beveled design. "Wow."

"Hmm...?" Ember asked.

Oops. She hadn't intended to say that out loud. "Oh, nothing.

Sorry I interrupted your shelf talk, but it sounds like the project will pick up some speed now."

"Hopefully, and you are never an interruption." Ember patted the box. "I love it when one of you brings me a box. It's like Christmas, and in your case..."

Holly laughed at the expectation in Ember's expression. She opened the flaps and set the mugs on the counter, delighted when Ember's eyes rounded in surprise.

Ember picked up one of the cups and turned it around in her hands. "This is really beautiful work. I knew you did some small porcelain ornaments and bells, but this..." She looked up. "Please tell me that this is a sample of something you want to display and sell."

"It is if you approve," Holly said.

"Absolutely. I think our Christmas shoppers will love them."

Holly smiled at her friend. "I hope—"

The bell over the door tinkled. Holly looked up and swallowed. Adonis was back, and he was looking straight at her.

CHAPTER TWO

The door to Crafted with Love swung shut behind Riley Soeurs with a soft chime. His gaze brushed across Ember before zeroing in on the younger woman standing next to her. He hesitated in the doorway while impressions registered in his brain almost faster than he could process them. Full high cheekbones, perfectly arched brows over intense brown eyes, long curls in a shade he'd put somewhere between chestnut and auburn, and a bright smile that simply lit up the room. When that smile turned into a puzzled frown, Riley jerked himself back to reality. His reason for returning to the shop was twofold. He wanted to talk to Ember about a Christmas gift for his mom, and he wanted the name...and possibly the phone number...of the other woman behind the counter. It was a bonus that she was still there, but staring at her as if she were the last can of soda on a shelf loaded with bottled water probably wouldn't win him any points. His long-legged stride carried him to the counter in a dozen steps.

"Back so soon?" Ember looked at her watch. "You've been gone less than ten minutes. Don't tell me you have plans to show me already."

Riley leaned against the counter, flashed the unknown beauty a smile, and directed his attention to Ember. "That'll take me at least an hour."

Ember crossed her arms and gave him what had to be her best don't-mess-with-me look.

"I'm joking. Your project will get the full complement of skills Dad so lovingly pounded into my head."

"Good to know. So what can I do for you?"

Riley jerked a thumb over his shoulder. "I came to ask about your Christmas stuff. You know my mom. She's crazy about that kind of thing. Once she's done decorating, it'll look like Santa's elves camped out in our living room for two weeks."

Ember crossed her arms, and Riley flinched under her stare.

"I know that your mother puts a great deal of thought and effort into making her home a cozy and tasteful place for her family to spend the holidays. It would be a shame if she found out that her eldest child was less than appreciative."

The threat was thinly veiled but good-natured. Riley held his hands up in a gesture of surrender. "We all love it, and she knows it. I came back to see if ornaments and small stuff is all your Christmas crafty person does. Scoring the perfect gift won't just make Mom happy, it'll earn me some serious points. I need all I can get."

"A man Christmas shopping before December twenty-third? What have you done now?" Ember asked.

Riley glanced at the younger woman. She'd smiled through their earlier banter. Now her expression was one of speculation. The last thing he wanted the beautiful stranger to carry away from this meeting was suspicion. "Not a thing, but it's never too late to plan for the future."

Ember's laugh filled the store. "Riley, your sense of humor is just one of the things I love about you. Now I can add impeccable timing to that list." She turned to the other woman and put a hand on her shoulder. "I've been remiss in my manners. Holly, I'd like you to meet Riley Soeurs. Riley, this is Holly Hoffman, fellow crafter and expert in all things Christmas. I'm sure she'll be happy to fix you up." The bell over the door chimed as two new customers entered the store. "You two get acquainted while I get back to work."

Riley stuck his hand out over the counter. He couldn't believe his luck. He'd wanted her name...he'd hoped for her number. That she was the person he needed to talk to about Mom's gift was an extra he hadn't expected and one he certainly didn't intend to waste. He answered her smile with one of his own as she took his hand in a firm grip.

"Nice to meet you, Holly." He paused as the coincidence of her name and occupation struck him. "Wait..." He tilted his head and looked at her through squinted eyes. "Holly?"

"That's me," She shrugged. "I'm Holly, and I make Christmas ornaments." Her grin was mischievous. "Some things are destiny, I guess." She glanced down at their still joined hands.

Riley released his grip and took a step back. "Sorry."

"Not a problem," she replied. "Now tell me how I can help you."

Riley swallowed, hard, at her innocent question. *Have dinner with me, marry me, have my children.*

He pushed his wish list to the back of his mind and concentrated on the here and now. "I've been working out-of-state for a couple of years. Couldn't make it home much, even for the holidays." That seemed par for the course when you were in the ministry. Holidays meant extra services and activities, not fewer. Services you were expected to attend. "Now that I'm home, I want to do something special for Mom. She loves Christmas, and she loves handmade, one-of-a-kind things." He pried his gaze from Holly's face...lovely even with a smudge of dirt on one cheek...and glanced around the shop. "This felt like the right place to start." His eyes met hers once again. "So tell me, Holly, keeper of all things Christmas. Can you help me?"

~

Could it be that easy? She'd had the Nativity set in her possession for less than two hours. Did she already have a sure customer on the line? Holly twisted a strand of her hair around a finger and chewed on her bottom lip. Getting the thing painted and sold wouldn't just ensure a merry Christmas for Riley's mom, but for her as well. First things first though. She had a price in her head, one she wouldn't back away from easily. Would he pay it?

She clasped her hands behind her back and tipped up on her toes. "I just acquired something you might be interested in. What were you looking to spend?"

"Hard to say without knowing what you're talking about."

"And that's a fact. Do you have time to wait while I run out to my car?"

He waved a hand toward the door in the back wall. "By all means. You have my curiosity stirred up now. Do you need some help?"

The fact that he offered only added to the appeal Holly was already feeling. Helpful as well as hunky. But she couldn't remember if any of the boxes had prices on them. The last thing she needed him to see was a twenty-five-dollar garage-sale sticker on something she planned to sell for much more. "Nope, just wait right here. I'll be back in a sec."

Holly made her way to the break room, left her coffee on the bar that divided the room, and snagged the cart parked next to the back door. She loaded the boxes onto the plastic shelves, carefully checking inside and out for stickers. There weren't any, but better safe than sorry. The angel was the last piece. As she held him, she couldn't help but notice how warm the porcelain was in her hands. Her puzzled gaze went to the back seat of the car and then lifted to the sky. It was a sunny day, and sunshine through car windows always magnified the heat, but had the other figures felt as warm? A small shiver ran up her spine.

Oh, get a grip!

The angel went back into its bed of protective shredded paper. What was it about this thing? This angel was beginning to give her the heebie-jeebies, and she couldn't afford that, especially now. As she replaced the lid, something fluttered, stopping her mid-motion. Her teeth clenched as she lifted the lid a second time.

Nothing moved.

Of course it didn't.

Holly gave it a few seconds, finally breathing a sigh of relief when a small puff of wind whispered into the alley and stirred the tiny bits of paper packed around the angel. *There you go, silly. Just the wind.* She replaced the lid and pushed the cart back into the store. Once inside she unboxed each of the figurines and arranged them on the table in the break room. She took a step back and admired them from several angles. They made a pretty display even in their unfinished condition. The trick now was to get Riley to see the same possibilities she saw.

She went to the door that led to the shop and peeked out. Riley was still there. Ruthie Gates, one of the other crafters, had come in for her afternoon shift and was keeping him company. Seemed Riley was known and loved by all.

Holly cleared her throat. When they both looked in her direction, she waved at Ruthie and then motioned for Riley to join her.

Riley gave Ruthie a quick hug before coming to meet Holly in the doorway. He made a great show of looking at his watch. "You are three hundred and sixty seconds over your estimate. Does that earn me a discount off this mystery price?"

"Sorry, no discounts, but I think..." Holly crossed her fingers behind her back. He had to like it. She was already choosing the color of her new car in her head. *Merry Christmas to me.* "You're gonna like this." With a hand on his arm, she led him to the table and stepped aside. When he didn't speak for several seconds, Holly rushed to explain.

"Of course, none of the pieces are finished yet. I was thinking blue and gold for the angel, brighter, richer colors for the wise man. But, if you're interested, I can do the pieces to order..." She stopped when Riley held up a hand. He circled the table, looking at the arrangement from every angle. When he reached for the angel,

Holly almost stopped him. Instead she watched his face to see if he felt anything out of the ordinary. Obviously not, since after examining it front and back, he placed it back on the table without a second's hesitation.

"Nice. What are they made out of?"

"Porcelain." Holly picked up the angel and held it to the light. "Watch." She waved a hand behind one of the wings. "See the shadow?"

"Yes."

"You don't get that with a ceramic piece. Ceramic is more dense." She replaced the figurine, crossed her arms, and waited.

"Perfect," he finally said. "In fact..." In a move that mimicked his father he pulled a tape measure and a small notebook from his back pocket, measured the angel, the tallest of the figurines, and made a note.

"What are you doing?"

Riley looked up at her. "Well, unless your price is seriously astronomical, I'm buying my mother a Christmas present, and while you're painting, I'll be building a crèche."

"A crèche?"

He made motions over the table with his hands. "You know...a stable...a barn... Something with an open front to display all of this in. It will have hay on the floor, maybe a lighted star on top. When this is all said and done, I'll have enough brownie points to get forgiveness for robbing a bank." Riley looked at Holly. "I'm not going to need to, am I?"

"Need to what?" Holly asked.

"Rob a bank." He waved at the table. "So that I can pay for this."

Giddiness bubbled up in Holly at his words. He saw it... He saw it just like she did. She rubbed her hands together. *The moment of truth.* "I don't think you'll need to break the law. I can have these finished for you and delivered in time for Christmas..." She swallowed and gave him a higher price than she really wanted. She'd bargain a little, make him feel like he was getting a deal. "Six hundred dollars." She stopped, took a deep breath and held it while he digested her words.

~

SIX HUNDRED DOLLARS? Riley whistled, looked at Holly, back to the Nativity set, and circled the table once more. He had the money, barely, and since he was living at home for the time being, his expenses were less than normal. Still...

Riley crossed his arms. Maybe she would come down a little. "That's pretty steep. I could probably do four-fifty without starving for the next month."

Holly mirrored his pose. Her chin up while she looked down her nose at him. Even though she was trying to rob him blind, he still found her adorable.

"This is going to eat up a lot of my time, you know."

"Yeah." He thought fast and realized... "But I figure having me as a sure buyer actually gives you a bit more time. If I buy it, you don't have to have it finished until mid-December. If you had to have it ready to display out there"—he motioned to the shop—"I'm guessing you'd need it a lot sooner, right?" He could tell by her expression that his logic had scored a direct hit.

"Five-fifty." Holly picked up one of the boxes on the cart, opened it, and reached for the corresponding figurine.

Oh, she was good, he'd have to give her that. Her actions more than signaled her intent. She was obviously ready to pack the set away without wasting one more second on a reluctant buyer who didn't recognize the value of her talent.

Riley picked up the angel and pretended to give it a more thorough going over. He put it down after several seconds and met Holly's determined gaze. "I'll meet you in the middle." He held out a hand. "Five hundred."

Riley held his breath while Holly considered his counter offer. He wanted this set...more, he wanted to spend time getting to know Holly. If he had to backpedal to the five-fifty price, he would, regardless of the damage it would do to his ego and his bank account. After an interminable wait, Holly took his proffered hand.

"Deal."

When she went to pull away, Riley held tighter. "On one condition."

Holly tilted her head in question.

"Have dinner with me tonight."

She disengaged her hand. "That sounds like fun, but I can't tonight. I still have one more job for the day. I won't get home until after seven."

Riley didn't intend to be brushed off that easily, and unless he missed his guess, there was a trace of disappointment in her voice. "Tomorrow then. I'll even let you pick the restaurant."

Holly didn't hesitate. "Now you have a deal. But I really need to hurry if I'm gonna get finished for the day."

Riley circled the table and picked up a box from the cart.

"What are you doing?" she asked.

"If I help you pack up and re-load your car, you get on your way faster, and I get a few more minutes of your company."

"I'll bet you think you're clever."

Riley nestled the angel into the largest box before taking the notebook and pen from his pocket. "Six-thirty OK for tomorrow?" When she nodded, he continued. "Write your address and phone number down for me." He whistled a snappy little tune while she did as he asked. He had the perfect gift for Mom at a price he could afford and a date with a beautiful woman. He'd take clever.

CHAPTER THREE

Holly burst through the door of the house she shared with her big sister, Sage. What a day this Friday had turned out to be. She needed to share or explode.

"Sage."

"Back here."

Holly followed the voice back to the last bedroom down the hall. Sage was just poking her head through the neck opening of a lightweight green sweater. She lifted her long red curls free with both hands and gave her head a shake. That was all it took for her sister's thick wavy curls to settle into a slightly messy style that Holly had spent her whole life trying and failing to replicate. Holly smothered a moment of sibling jealousy.

When Holly looked in the mirror every morning, she saw a passable face best described as *cute*. Sage was nothing short of beautiful. Holly's hair was long and naturally curled into tight ringlets. Sage's hair had the luster and body that every shampoo commercial on the planet promised but failed to deliver. Good genes couldn't be bottled. Holly was short and petite and often snarky. Sage was two years older, four inches taller, with flawlessly proportioned curves, and sweetness rolled off her in waves. She'd be easy to hate if Holly didn't love her so much.

"Wow, you're really late tonight. Busy day?" Sage asked.

Holly leaned against the door frame. "This day just might go down as one of the most productive days of my life."

"Do tell." Sage moved to her jewelry box sitting on top of her chest of drawers and perused the contents with a frown.

Holly joined her. She looked from the ruthlessly organized collection to her sister and back before lifting a long gold chain from its compartment. "This one. It will really stand out against the green."

Sage didn't question the choice. She fastened it around her neck and studied the result in the mirror. After straightening a small kink in the chain, she nodded at her reflection before finally facing her sister. "Details, girl, details." Sage took Holly's hand and pulled her to the side of the bed. She sat on the edge of the mattress with one leg tucked beneath her. "I have fifteen minutes. Tell me why this day was so special."

"Where do you have to be in fifteen minutes?" Holly asked instead.

"There's a single adult mixer at Grace Community tonight. Pizza and a Bible study followed by a movie in the gym."

The good news Holly'd been so excited to share took a backseat to confusion. This religion thing Sage was so wrapped up in lately was getting out of control. "You're going back to church...tonight?"

"I'd call it more of a party, but it's at the church, so...yeah."

Holly folded her arms. "You were gone half the day on Sunday. You went to service on Wednesday night, and you invited me to some lady's thing in the morning. Tonight, too?"

"You want to come?" Sage asked. "I'll wait for you to get ready."

"We've had this conversation. You've gone off the deep end. I'm not jumping in after you."

A flicker of sadness crossed Sage's face. "I know you don't get it, but you might if you gave it a chance."

Holly shook her head. She was out of words.

Sage exhaled, looked at her watch, and took Holly's hand. A

brilliant smile replaced the sadness. "We're wasting time. I want to hear about your day before I leave."

~

HOLLY STOOD at the door and watched Sage's taillights fade in the distance. Something strange tugged at her heart. Some half-formed desire to get in her Jeep, follow her sister back to Garfield, and see what all the church fuss was about.

She snorted as she turned from the door. She and Sage shared the same parents, upbringing, and life lessons. That life had taught Holly one very important lesson. Depend on your own wits for what you want. That lesson had served her well over the years. Hard work filled the void in Holly's life. She liked it that way. Sage worked hard too. If she'd found an additional way to bring some balance into her life, more power to her. That didn't mean that Holly had to follow in her footsteps.

Holly's stomach rumbled, reminding her of how much time had passed since lunch. She shook off thoughts of Sage and her inexplicable church attendance and went to the kitchen to see what she could find. A survey of the leftovers in the fridge yielded several options. She bypassed the stew Sage had made over the weekend as well as the remnants of a Mexican casserole and settled on a plate of meatloaf and macaroni and cheese. No denying it was comfort food, but it would heat up nice and quick in the microwave.

As tired as she was, she still wanted to get a start on the Nativity set tonight. She had an image in her head of how the angel would look when it was finished, and the sooner she got started, the sooner that vision would come to life.

Come to life?

The words brought up impossible images of porcelain wings waving in the breeze and folded hands that should be lifted. The memory made her gulp the bite she was chewing. A fit of coughing bent Holly over as the food clumped in her throat. She straightened, then chugged a drink of her iced tea and thumped her breastbone with the heel of her hand, gasping as the obstruction cleared. She slid down in her chair, leaned her head against the backrest, and allowed her hands to hang loose at her sides while she took in a couple of calming breaths.

And that's enough of that. Holly pushed her half-eaten dinner aside and surged to her feet. Determined steps carried her out the back door and into the garage she and Sage used as a shared workspace. Her finger trembled as she jabbed at the button that raised the door, her mind racing as she assigned adjectives to the way she'd reacted to the angel that day.

Stupid.

Ridiculous.

Absurd.

Holly lifted the largest of the boxes from the backseat of the Jeep and carried it back to her workspace. This nonsense ended right now. Before opening the box, she retrieved her collection of porcelain paints and selected the clear glaze she wanted for the wings. She'd give the wings a quick glaze and put the thing in the kiln overnight. Heating at over two thousand degrees, those wings would be baked to an immovable finish by the time she got back to her project tomorrow.

With the kiln preheating and the timer set, she laid out her paints, lifted the lid of the box, and removed the angel from its packing.

"You know it's not going to be that easy, right?"

Holly fumbled the figurine, catching it just before it crashed onto the table. Her hands trembled as she set it upright and bent down to study it almost nose to nose. As her heartbeat slowly returned to normal, she chided herself for the dozenth time in as many hours. Porcelain figurines didn't move. They certainly didn't talk.

"But I'm not your everyday glass angel, Holly. My name is Gabriel, and we've been sent to tell you a story."

Holly clutched the table as the edges of her vision blurred.

Once the world settled, she had just enough presence of mind to turn the kiln off and smack the button to lower the garage door as she fled into the house.

She was exhausted. Yes, that was it. She'd been working too hard over the last few weeks, and it had caught up with her. Holly raced to her bedroom, slammed the door, and turned the lock. An early bedtime and a good night's sleep were what she needed. The world would be back to normal in the morning.

RILEY ROSE from behind the coffee table, his hands curved into claws, his mouth stretched into a ferocious mask. "Roarrrr!"

The screams of his four-year-old twin siblings were loud enough to shake the walls of the house. Where seconds ago, they had been *hunters* on the search for big game, they'd quickly done an about-face and fled the field of battle. Riley went from hunted to hunter as he chased them down the hall. Zach stopped outside his bedroom, a previously designated safe zone, and screamed at Aimee.

"Hurry, the lion is about to eat you."

Aimee risked one look behind her and dove through the door just before Zach slammed it closed in Riley's face.

The windows rattled from the concussion.

Riley spent a few seconds on his hands and knees scratching at the door while making loud snuffling noises and low growls. Whispers and giggles filtered through the door, and he knew it was just a matter of time before the door opened and the chase began anew. He might be twenty years older than the twins, but after growing up as the only child in a restrictive home, he was having just as much fun as they were. The fun ended when he felt the sting of a snapped dishtowel on his hindquarters. He turned to see his mother rolling the towel for a second shot.

"Hey."

"Hey, yourself." Mom flipped the towel. This time the shot landed on his shoulder. "Play dead."

Riley retreated to the corner, sat on one wound, and rubbed the other. "What was that for?"

His mom straightened and put her hands on her hips. Her face struggled against a smile, despite the intimidating posture. "You three are raising the roof. I'm trying to cook dinner, and I can't hear myself think. I don't know which is worse. Two four-year-olds, or three."

"Three?"

The smile finally won. "Yes, three. It's hard to tell my children apart when you're all running around the house like maniacs." She stepped around him and opened the door to Zach's room.

Riley could see the twins sitting on the edge of Zach's bed, a mound of rolled up socks between them as ammunition. "Roarrr." The sound that came out of Riley's throat was half laugh, half growl. It was enough to send a hail of the soft projectiles through the door. Most of them bounced off their mother.

Mom glanced over her shoulder and pinned him to the wall with a harsh glare. "Riley Austin Soeurs."

He hunched down and pressed his lips together. Most kids, regardless of their age, knew what it meant when a parent played the three-name card. Riley was no exception. "Sorry," he whispered, hoping she didn't hear the amusement in the word.

Mom spoke to the twins again. "Dinner is almost ready. Daddy will be home soon. I need you guys to clean this mess and get washed up."

"We're lion hunters," Aimee said, lifting a second round of ammunition.

"I killed the lion. You're safe." Mom stooped down, gathered a half dozen pair of socks, and tossed them into the room. "Get a move on. Riley will play Candy Land with you guys after dinner." She closed the door on their cheers.

Riley followed her down the hall and into the kitchen. "Why did you promise them that? I hate that game. They cheat."

"Yes, but they do it quietly. I spent my day at the spa shouting workout instructions like a crazed drill sergeant. I've earned a little quiet, don't you think?" She returned to the stove, tossed the towel-turned-weapon over her shoulder, and stirred a large pot of chili.

Riley found a clean spoon and dipped it into the thick red mixture. He blew on his bite and tasted. "Needs more salt."

As his mom sprinkled and stirred, Riley leaned against the counter. "I met someone interesting today. You probably know her. Holly Hoffman?"

"I do know her. She's one of Ember's crafters. Her Christmas ornaments are pieces of art. I've already bought several for our tree this year."

Riley gave himself a mental pat on the back. Not only had he secured the perfect Christmas gift, but he was working with someone whose work his mom appreciated. *Double points.* "What can you tell me about her?"

His mom's expression turned thoughtful as she stirred. "She's quite pretty. But you probably already determined that for yourself."

"You'd be correct there. She's gorgeous."

Mom nodded. "I haven't talked to her a lot, mostly just about the things I've purchased. She's a very talented crafter, and she's independent as well as industrious. I'd almost compare her to Dane in that regard."

"How do you mean?"

"Oh"—his mom made a vague motion in the air—"you know the motto on Dane's van? No task too big. No job too small. That's Holly. She doesn't have a job in the traditional sense...like nine-to-five, five days a week. She pursues several small things to make her ends meet. She's always trying something new. I love her sweet disposition, but if you look and listen, you'll catch hints of something sad hidden in her heart, something..." She tilted her head as if searching for the right word. "...wounded. I wouldn't call her an introvert, but there's an underlying shyness about her that Sage doesn't share."

"Sage?"

"Holly's older sister. Sage is the more outspoken one of the two. I've gotten to know her a little better since she started attending Grace Community Church a few weeks ago."

"But Holly...?"

Mom looked at him, her expression full of amusement. "Holly is twenty-three, her favorite color is green. I suspect that might have something to do with the whole Christmas thing. She loves coffee—I rarely see her without a cup close at hand—and she doesn't get her nails done."

Riley frowned at his mother. "That's an odd piece of information."

"You asked me what I know, so I'm telling you. One of the jobs she has is selling cosmetics. There was a pricy face cream I wanted to try, and I offered to do her nails several times in exchange for the cream. She said no thanks because pretty nails and house cleaning didn't go together. Now, why the twenty questions?"

"I'm taking her to dinner tomorrow night," Riley said. "I wanted a bit of a head start."

The door slammed in the other room. "I'm home," Dane called.

"Dinner is ready when you are." Mom scooted past Riley and took a stack of bowls from the cabinet. She ladled chili into each one. "A date, huh? Well then the most important piece of advice I can give you is to guard your heart. Holly isn't a believer. Sage is working on that, but she hasn't had any luck."

Riley mulled those words as his mom left the kitchen to welcome Dane home and fetch the twins.

Guard his heart?

He frowned. Good advice, but something told him it might have come too late.

CHAPTER FOUR

After her traumatic Friday night, Holly slept late Saturday morning. When her eyes finally fluttered open, her bedroom was bright with early fall sunlight. She raised her hands over her head for a fingertip-to-toe stretch, taking the time to savor every relaxed muscle in her body. The action was cut short when her nose picked up the warm, toasty scent of freshly brewed coffee. She sort of remembered hearing Sage moving around in her room across the hall earlier. Considering the time and the thirty-mile drive back to Garfield, her sister was likely long gone to her church thing, but she'd made coffee. Her big sis was thoughtful like that.

Holly rolled from the bed, stood, and crossed to the window. A quick look through the blinds confirmed what the bright light in the room had already promised. A brilliant blue sky with not a single cloud in sight. It promised to be a productive day and a perfect evening.

A perfect evening?

The thought sent prickles of anticipation up Holly's spine. She had a date with the handsome Riley Soeurs tonight. Her bootie shook in a little happy dance as she wiggled into her jeans and pulled on a paint-stained T-shirt. Stopping in front of the mirror, she smiled and addressed her reflection.

"Girl, you scored. He's a hottie. He's not only hot but thoughtful and funny right along with it." The corners of Holly's mouth ticked up when she remembered yesterday's little bidding war. He hadn't been fooled by her for a second, nor she by him. Getting to know him better was going to be an interesting journey.

She ran a brush through her hair and bundled the unruly mass into a tail at the nape of her neck while continuing her one-sided conversation. "What do you think? Should we invite him in after dinner to take a look at the day's progress on the Nativity set?" Before the whispered question had a chance to fade into the air, her anticipation turned to apprehension, and Holly's playful mood morphed into a stomach full of hot nerves.

She glanced at the bedroom door with an audible gulp. Her mind's eye traveled down the hall and out into the garage where it landed on the object of her anxiety. She couldn't have stopped the cold chill that skittered through her extremities with an electric blanket set on maximum heat.

Come on, Holly. You were tired and punchy yesterday. Porcelain angels don't talk.

In an act of sanity-preserving defiance, Holly threw the door wide, marched straight to the garage, and picked the angel up in both hands.

"What have you got to say for yourself?"

It was cool and still and silent in her grasp. Relief whooshed out of her. Her laugh was nervous, but her hands were steadier when she set the figurine back on the table. She unboxed the rest of the manger pieces and arranged them on the work surface. A critical study yielded nothing out of the ordinary.

"Good." Holly spoke the assurance aloud and found it helped to reinforce the normalcy of the moment. "It's all good." She headed back to the kitchen for her first hit of morning caffeine, satisfied that she'd have positive progress to share with Riley later. The Nativity set was important to both of them, and she didn't think he'd be too impressed if her report came in the form of a boxful of pulverized white shards.

After downing a toasted bagel slathered in veggie-blend cream cheese, Holly poured a second cup of coffee into her large work mug, doctored it with sugar and cocoa-caramel creamer, and returned to the garage. She pulled a wheeled chair close to the table and set up a TV tray on either side. One was for her paints, the other for her drink. She'd learned early on, and tragically, that her drinks didn't belong on her work surface. Once she'd assembled brushes, paint thinner, and a glass tile to use as a color mixing palette, she was ready to begin.

Her hands were steady as she picked up the angel. "Come to Mama, Gabe. Let's get acquainted."

"I prefer Gabriel. The Heavenly Host has never been big on nicknames."

The angel clattered back to the surface of the table as Holly yanked her hands away.

"Careful. I'm very fragile in this incarnation."

Holly rubbed at her eyes as the angel's wings stretched one at a time as if checking for damage. Saliva pooled in her mouth when the porcelain arms lowered to raise the hem of the tunic. She shoved herself away from the table when the figure stooped slightly and looked at sandaled feet she hadn't even known were under there.

"If you break me, you won't hear the story *and* you won't get your money."

"You have feet." She snapped her mouth shut. Of all the strange things happening right now, that was the thing that got her attention...feet?

The angel's face lifted, and the colorless eyes seemed to stare into Holly's. "Of course, how else could I stand?"

"But you...I mean...how...?" Holly lowered her head and massaged her temples.

Surely, despite what her ears and eyes were telling her, when she looked again, things would be normal. But when her gaze returned to the table, not only was the angel watching her, but the cow was chewing some invisible something, and Mary was rocking the infant. "This just isn't possible. I can't—"

Gabriel's upraised hand stopped her. "I think we got off to a bad start, and I blame myself for that. I was afraid you were going to walk right by us yesterday. I called to you and waved to get your attention. I'm sorry if I frightened you. We aren't here to hurt you or cause you any trouble."

Holly remembered the odd voice she couldn't locate yesterday. "That was you?"

The figurine of Mary stood and kissed the baby on his head before passing him to Joseph. Then, she took a step forward. She grabbed one of the angel's delicate looking wings and pulled him back a couple of steps. "He's a pro at scaring people. Why, I almost dropped my water pitcher the day he sprang up out of nowhere to speak to me." She lifted a hand to her mouth as if to stop herself from sharing too much. "But that's part of the story for later."

"Yeah," the shepherd piped up. "He was front and center the night he and his friends lit up the midnight sky outside of Bethlehem. Knocked us all right to the ground. I thought we were going to die."

The angel cleared his throat. "We're in danger of getting ahead of ourselves, and I still need to explain."

Holly blinked. When she refocused, all the figurines except the angel stood motionless and back in their original positions and postures.

"I know you have questions," Gabriel said. "I promise they will all be answered. First of all, I want you to know that you aren't losing your mind. This is all very real."

Holly's head was shaking before he got the final word out. "Impossible."

"And donkeys don't talk, and fish don't swallow people, and virgins don't have babies."

Holly choked back her next comment when the angel scored a direct hit using her own thoughts from the previous day.

"With God, all things are possible." His wave took in the figurines surrounding him. "Even this."

As the angel talked, Holly's nerves began to settle. He had a pleasant voice, and despite the outrageous situation, she believed him when he said they meant her no harm. The whole thing was kind of cool in a *Twilight Zone*, warped sort of way.

Her brain kicked into gear as speculation bloomed. Holly had a gold mine in front of her. Riley wasn't going to be happy with her, and she already regretted that, but there was no way she was turning loose of this set for a measly five hundred dollars.

Gabriel continued. "We've been sent to tell you the story of the Christ child's birth."

Holly snorted. "I think you got the wrong sister. I don't believe in all that religious hocus pocus. Sage—"

"Your sister has made her own connection with our Savior. Our story is for you. Before we get started, there are some ground rules you need to understand." The expression on the angel's face turned shrewd. "We are not a parlor act. And before you ask, no, I can't read your mind, but avarice seems to be the common knee-jerk reaction to the unusual, so before you start plotting how to capitalize on this, you ought to know that no one can hear us except you. No one can perceive our movements except you. Once our story is told and your painting is complete, we will return to being nothing more than the porcelain figurines you purchased."

Holly mentally downgraded her upcoming vehicle purchase back from the Lexus LX of her dreams to the Buick Encore of her budget.

If Gabriel saw her expression, he ignored it. He turned his attention to the paint laid out on the table. "If that blue is what you have in mind for my robe, I heartily agree. I'm ready to get started when you are." With that pronouncement, the angel raised his hands and resumed his stately pose.

Holly lifted him from the table with tentative hands, still not quite believing but no longer afraid. She dipped the brush into the blue paint and made a long stroke down the front of the robe. She paused when the sound of laughter filled her head.

"You're fine. I've never been tickled before."

Holly snorted. Not only did she have the world's only talking porcelain angel. She had the world's only ticklish porcelain angel. But...she'd heard his voice, but his mouth hadn't moved. "How'd you do that?"

"Do what?"

"This...that talking in my head thing."

"I assumed you would rather not work with a moving target. While you work, we will talk heart to heart."

That the angel could speak directly to her heart seemed impossible, but then, it *was* a talking porcelain figurine. Apparently *impossible* no longer applied.

Holly made a few more careful swipes with the brush. Her movements became more defined once she was certain the laughter was over.

"My story begins on the day I was called to the Father's throne."

Your father? She responded in her head and stopped. He'd assured her that he couldn't read her mind. But if he could hear dialog aimed at him, how could she be sure he couldn't access something else? This was weird enough without the fear of these things rummaging around in her thoughts. She repeated the words aloud. "Your father is a king?"

"God, the Father and Creator of all things."

"Um... Right...." She drew the word out, not bothering to mask her cynical tone.

"All of Heaven knew that the time for the Messiah was drawing close. God always keeps His promises, even those four thousand years in the making."

Holly refreshed the paint on her brush and maintained her silence. The only thing more bizarre than having a conversation with a figurine would be arguing with one. She concentrated on painting one of the folds of the robe instead.

"I wasn't surprised to receive the summons. One of my

colleagues had been dispatched to earth six months earlier. We all knew that there was a second message to deliver. I entered the throne room, went down on one knee, and bowed my head. "Yes, My Lord."

"It's time."

Holly's brush paused in mid-stroke. The new voice resonated in her head and bunched her shoulders with its authoritative tone.

"I stand ready to do Your bidding," I said.

"And I trust no one else with this sacred duty. You will find the young woman in the countryside outside of the city of Nazareth. Her name is Mary. She is a direct descendant of King David."

"The Lord God bowed His head for a second, and when He looked at me again, I was not surprised to see a trace of sadness on His face. Just as we all knew the time for this message was at hand, we all knew that there would be great suffering before the final rejoicing."

"Be cautious in your approach as she has led a sheltered life. Your message will surprise her, but she will believe. She has been taught and prepared for this moment her whole life."

"I will do my best, My Lord."

"You have everything you need?"

"Yes."

"Then prepare to depart at once with My blessing."

A few moments of silence passed while Holly painted. She'd done her best to filter out the words in her head. The figurine would have to be fired in the kiln overnight before another color could be added, so she wanted to get as much of the blue done today as she could. Holding the angel by an unpainted wing she reached for a small turntable. After setting the statue in the middle she gave it a gentle spin, inspecting for places she'd missed.

"There's one." She put out a hand, stopped the motion, and touched the brush to the tiny bare spot next to the sash.

"Whoa." The angel's wings fluttered as if fighting for balance. The tip of the brush skittered across the sash, leaving a blue smear where it didn't need to be.

Holly sat back with a jerk. "I thought you were going to be still while I worked."

"That was my intent," Gabriel said. "I didn't expect you to put me on some out-of-control amusement park ride."

Holly reached for a rag and the container of paint remover. "Out of control? Good grief." She dabbed at the smear with the cloth, yanking it away when the angel shivered. "What's wrong now?"

"It's cold."

She put her head in her hands. "Are all angels such crybabies?"

The angel straightened to his full twelve inches. "I am an archangel of the Most High God."

"Mm-hmm." She inspected the repair, happy to see that no permanent damage had been done. "You do understand that I'm about to bake you in a hot kiln for several hours?"

"Provision has been made for that. Since you will not be available for conversation during that time, I shall depart this confining embodiment for the duration of the process. I will return once it is finished."

"Lucky me," Holly muttered before getting up to turn on the kiln. When she turned back to the table, the *gang* had come to life once more and surrounded the angel. For a second Holly felt more than a little outnumbered.

Gabriel took a step forward. When he spoke, his voice rang with an authority that had been missing before. "Holly Hoffman, you are not lucky. You are blessed. The God of all Creation has a plan for your life. A wondrous future lies ahead if you would but follow that plan. We are divine messengers sent to show you the way."

"You spin a great yarn, Gabe, but I outgrew fairy tales a long time ago." Without waiting for the preheat cycle to complete, Holly opened the kiln and slid the angel inside. She looked at him through the opening as the increasing heat washed over her face and paused as something prodded at her consciousness. It was the same uncomfortable feeling she got when Sage tried to share the details of her newfound Christianity. It was a longing to have something besides herself to depend on. Something...bigger.

But that was foolish. She'd worked herself into a good place through hard, honest effort. The thought of some invisible God lounging around on a cloud, playing chess with the lives of humans, didn't do a thing for her. With a deep breath, Holly closed the door, latched it, and spun away. She had an Avon order to work on, a week's worth of laundry to do, and a date with a hot new guy. "My future isn't in anyone's hands but my own, and that's where I plan to keep it."

CHAPTER FIVE

Saturday might seem like an odd day to start a new job, but Riley was out the door and headed to Ashton's food bank long before the rest of the house began to stir. He'd accepted the position of outreach pastor at Calvary Worship Church late last week but he'd yet to see the facility he'd be in charge of. That was scheduled to happen on Monday morning, but something was urging him to get a head start, and it felt like more than simple curiosity. Experience had taught him that when the Spirit nudged, you moved.

Located just seven miles north of Garfield, Ashton boasted more than four times the population of Garfield along with a thriving college. The homeless and indigent population was growing right along with the town. Calvary Worship aimed to have a positive impact on those numbers. Riley was proud to take the helm of the food bank, one arm of that ministry.

Riley unlocked the front door to the Bread Basket and stepped into a good-sized reception area with folding chairs lining one wall and a row of shopping carts parked against the one opposite. A large desk sat against the short back wall and held little more than a phone, a computer, and a few standard office supplies. He knew from the briefing he'd received last week that this area was used by volunteers for client screening before they were granted access to the store. His eyes shifted to the door next to the desk. Per that briefing his new office lay on the other side. As eager as he was to see and organize his space, he chose the wide door located just beyond the row of carts instead.

Here, the bright overhead lights gleamed off the store's spotless tile floor. The hum from the refrigeration units was oddly loud in the unoccupied building. He lifted his nose and sniffed. He couldn't see any produce from where he stood, but the citrusy tang in the air told him the center's clients would have a decent selection. A leisurely stroll took him through four long aisles stacked generously with cans, boxes, jars, and bags. The fifth row contained produce, dairy, and frozen foods.

A display of red delicious apples caught his gaze. He hadn't taken time for breakfast, and the bright red fruit proved too much for his willpower to resist. He plucked one from the neat stack, buffed it against his shirt, and took a healthy bite. While he chewed, he turned in a circle and counted his blessings. Not only was he in charge of the day-to-day running of the facility, but he hoped that there would be opportunities over the months ahead to partner with some of the other churches in the area as they worked to minister to the needs of Ashton and the smaller towns that surrounded it, places like Garfield and Cable.

Riley swallowed and bowed his head.

Thank you, God. Not only have You allowed me to come home, but this is going to provide me with some invaluable ministry experience. You know I'm brand new at this. I need You to go before me with wisdom and direction. That odd sense of urgency washed over him again. Riley kept his eyes closed for several seconds, waiting for something to solidify, but nothing came.

With the apple in one hand and a heart full of anticipation, Riley made his way back through the store and the staging area and took his first look at his new office. He was pleasantly surprised to find that it was more spacious than he'd hoped for. The room was deeper than it was wide, with a bank of narrow windows high on the east wall. The green-tinted glass was thick and dingy with age. Regardless the natural light flooding through brightened the room and kept it from feeling like a cave. Riley crossed the room and attempted to assess the view to the outside world. He was six feet tall, but the bottom edge of the windows was even with his eyebrows. A boost to his tiptoes still didn't allow him to see out.

The apple core went into the trash as his attention shifted to the business aspects of the room. A couple of tall filing cabinets occupied the space next to the windows, and a large desk with a comfortable-looking chair sat in one corner. *Now we're talking.* Riley went around the desk and took the chair for a test drive. The leather creaked under his weight, and the bearings in the base squeaked as he twisted from left to right, but as he looked out over what he could now call his own, he couldn't help but feel incredibly blessed.

He rubbed his hands together, suddenly eager for more than just a look around. There had to be something he could do to get a head start on the upcoming week. He studied the computer on his desk. *Maybe...* He jiggled the mouse. The screen came up and requested a password to continue. Disappointing but not surprising.

His gaze went to the filing cabinets, but before he had a chance to open the first drawer, a racket drew him to the entry of his office where he could see the front door.

A man stood outside, alternately knocking and peering through the glass with his face pressed against the door. "Hello. I saw the car out front. Are you open?" The knocking resumed. "Is anyone in there? Hello."

Riley studied his unexpected visitor from the shadows of his office. The man had on a worn T-shirt tucked into frayed jeans that looked two or three sizes too large. They would have fallen down around his ankles if not for the belt cinched tight around his skinny waist. A cigarette smoldered between the fingers of one hand while the other banged on the door. A tattered duffle bag lay at his feet.

From his bald head and the bushy beard, Riley assumed his age at somewhere in his fifties.

The man took a step back and tried the handle, pushing and pulling, shaking his head in obvious frustration. "Please, if you're in there, open the door."

That's your cue, son.

As soon as Riley stepped into the shaft of light shining through the glass door, the pounding intensified.

"I told Cindy there was someone here. I told her so. She said you wouldn't help us, but I knew you would."

Riley crossed the room and turned the lock to open the door a crack. He took a deep breath and regretted it instantly. The stench that rolled off the stranger was rife with old smoke and body odor, a combination that threatened to reboot the apple he'd just finished. Riley swallowed and tried to disguise the urge to barf with a cough.

The old man frowned. He had moist, rheumy eyes that watched Riley as he took a long draw off the cigarette. The mouth behind the beard contained not a single tooth. He leaned into Riley's space. "Cat got your tongue, boy?"

Riley stepped back from the fog of smoke, fanning the air in front of his face.

The old man took the hint. "Sorry." He took a final drag, turned his head to exhale, and ground the glowing tip out on the side of the building. Once he was satisfied that the cigarette was out, he dropped the nub into his shirt pocket. He patted it. "Waste not, want not."

Riley's heart ached with the familiar empathy that had drawn him into the ministry. The stranger's athletic shoes were so ragged that Riley could see bare skin in several places. The inexplicable urge he'd felt all morning was becoming clearer with each shallow breath he took.

The old man held out a hand stained brown with nicotine and things Riley didn't want to think about too deeply. "I'm Gilbert Hoffman."

Riley clasped the filthy hand. "I'm..." He paused for a second while his new title rattled around in his head, but it wouldn't quite come together in his mouth. With a swallow, he tried again and managed to get it out. "I'm Pastor Riley." Just saying the words straightened his shoulders.

The old man peered at Riley through squinted eyes. "A pastor, heh?" He tilted his head while he scratched at a crusty ear. "Ain't you sort of young for that kinda thing?"

"No, sir." Riley's thoughts took a momentary detour as Gilbert's last name finally registered. *Hoffman.* A relation to Holly? He'd have to ask her. "What can I do for you today?"

"I live over yonder." Gilbert jabbed a thumb over his shoulder. "Me and Cindy. Cindy's my wife. We just moved into town last week. Got us a sweet little place over by the bowling alley. Supposed to be seven hundred dollars a month, but our section-eight housing allowance pays most of that, and the rent includes all our utilities." He dug in his pocket for his wallet and withdrew a plastic card and held it in front of Riley's face. "This ain't no credit card. This is my debit card. I'm on disability." He tapped his right eye. "I don't see real good."

Riley could tell from the rambling speech and the glut of information that an eye problem wasn't Gilbert's only issue. There'd been a neighbor back in the community where he'd grown up who was born with a developmental handicap. When it came to the details of his life, the guy had no social filter. He was just as likely to tell you how many trips he made to the bathroom each day as what he had for breakfast. Riley had no way of knowing if the handicap was genetic or just a byproduct of the life Gilbert had lived, but the problem was obvious if you looked and listened.

Gilbert continued. "It's getting on to the end of the month, and we don't get paid or get our food stamps for a week or so. When I saw a car out front, I thought you were open. All me and Cindy have in the house is a box of crackers. Can you help us?"

Riley ran a hand through his hair, not sure how to handle this situation. There was probably a guideline for emergency aid, but he hadn't been briefed on the finer points yet. "I was just working on some business stuff. We aren't open until Monday."

The old man's countenance fell, hope replaced with desperation. "Please, Pastor, you're here. Cindy's been real sick. We don't have money for her medicine till we get our check, but if I could feed her, I think she'd feel better. We don't need a lot. Maybe just a can of soup to go with the crackers."

Gilbert's pleading words nearly broke Riley's heart. He wasn't officially in charge yet, but he refused to make the old man beg, and there was no way he'd send him away hungry. He'd trained for ministry, and this was what it was all about. If the powers-that-be at Calvary Worship had a problem with the decision he was about to make, it was better that he knew about it up front. Because if they did, they weren't the sort of church he wanted to work for. He stepped out of the entry and held the door open. "Gilbert, I bet we can do a lot better than a can of soup. Come with me."

"God bless you, Pastor." Gilbert stepped inside and stood silently as Riley grabbed the nearest shopping cart and pushed it through the door into the store.

Riley looked at him over his shoulder. "You coming?"

The older man nodded. A few quick steps brought him even with the cart.

There were cards attached to the shelves indicating how many selections of each type of food were allowed per customer. Riley ignored them. He waved a hand at the loaded shelves. "Get what you need to last you until you get paid."

When Gilbert looked at him, tears were collecting in the corners of his eyes. "Pastor, I don't want to get you in no trouble. Just show me where you keep the soup, and I'll be on my way."

Riley took the lead from the reluctant older man, placing a couple of bags of breakfast cereal in the cart before reaching for a box of oatmeal. "Do you have a Bible?"

Instead of answering right away, Gilbert studied the selection of cereals. He took Riley's choices out of the cart and replaced them with a bag of corn flakes and a chocolate crispy rice. "These get nice and soft in the milk. Some things are hard to eat with no teeth." He offered a toothless smile. "A Bible?" He tapped his eye. "I have one, but I don't read so good. Cindy gets headaches when she reads."

"Got ya." Riley gave the basket a nudge and moved on to the bread. "There is a piece of Scripture in James that says that if a person comes to us needing food or clothing and we send them away with a verbal blessing instead of meeting their needs in a physical fashion, we've failed."

Gilbert tilted his head as if trying to take the words in. "It really says that in the Bible?"

"It really does. I'm not in the mood to fail today." Riley nodded at the loaves of bread. "Can you eat sandwiches?"

The next thirty minutes were spent loading the cart with everything from cereal to the requested soup to toilet paper. Once they pushed the cart back to the staging area, Riley took a hard look at the stack of groceries and thought about transportation for the first time. How was Gilbert supposed to get this stuff home?"

Your car is parked out front.

Riley nodded at the gentle reminder, more convinced than ever that the urge to come to the center that morning had been driven by something much larger than his curiosity. He looked at Gilbert and took a deep breath. The aroma wafting off the man had not improved, and Riley was supposed to pick Holly up for dinner later. If he took Gilbert home, his car would smell like a sewer. There didn't seem to be a way around that though.

"Wait right here." Riley stepped back into the store and switched off the lights. He did the same to his office and came back to find Gilbert loading items into his ripped tote. "You'll never fit all of that in there. Where did you say you lived?"

"Over by the bowling alley."

"That's right. Just a second." Riley sprinted to the back room and returned with two large boxes. "Let's load your stuff into these, and I'll drive you home."

"I've imposed on you too much already."

"You have not been an imposition. I'm pretty sure you're the reason God woke me up this morning. Let's get this stuff into my car."

Cindy's sick.

"Yep," Riley muttered before he asked Gilbert, "Did I hear you say you needed to pick up a prescription?"

"Can't 'till we get paid."

"Remember that verse I told you about?" Riley continued when Gilbert nodded. "I guess it goes for medicine as well as food."

And shoes.

Riley jerked his gaze heavenward. Shoes? He did a mental accounting of the cash he had in his wallet and hoped Holly liked hamburgers.

CHAPTER SIX

Holly was ready and waiting impatiently for Riley by six. If she could get out of the house and put the disturbing work on the Nativity set behind her, maybe, just maybe, she could save her sanity. Earlier this afternoon, once she'd finished her laundry, she'd made a second venture out to the garage while the angel was captive in the kiln. She figured she'd be safe if she worked on one of the animals.

Gabriel had said that he and his companions were there to tell her the Christmas story. That had to mean the human characters, Holly'd reasoned. The cow might have animated itself earlier, but it hadn't spoken. If angels existed, and it was getting harder and harder to deny that they might, she supposed it was normal that they spoke.

Cows didn't talk, and even if they did, what sort of a story would they tell? She was grasping at straws. She didn't care. She hadn't been prepared for how wrong she could be.

The instant she lifted the figurine, her mind flooded with images that were as vivid as any of the angel's words.

If it were possible to have too much information about a cow, Holly could now claim that privilege as her own.

Clover...that was the cow's name...had lived a contented life as the single milk cow of an innkeeper in Bethlehem. Well cared for and treated like a pet by her master's many children, she shared the stable with an assortment of sheep, goats, and chickens. Food was plentiful, the stable was warm, and life was good. It was about to get worse and better all in the same night.

The mental pictures that coalesced in Holly's mind were as effective as words. She experienced the disturbance of having her small space invaded by a strange donkey and its two weary humans. The confusion as she was moved out of her stall to make room for the woman to rest. The cries a few hours later as the woman struggled to give birth. Clover's resentment as her manger was hijacked to give the squalling child a place to lie. She would get no hay or grain as long as this baby occupied her space. Bitterness that turned to wonder as she listened to the humans talk.

Was the child that lay sleeping in her hay really a king? Not just a king, but a ruler come to save the world? The thought was beyond her comprehension, and things only grew more confusing as a group of shepherds crowded into the narrow space.

Clover edged closer as the couple settled in for the rest of the night. She studied the tiny human, sniffed him gently from head to toe, and even touched the tip of her tongue to the exposed head of downy hair.

While his exhausted parents slept, the baby's eyes opened in the soft light of dawn and met Clover's curious stare. Clover felt a burst of pride as the look seemed to communicate the truth of everything she'd heard the humans say.

The cow's low sound of homage seemed to echo in Holly's throat. *Welcome to Bethlehem, Your Majesty. I'm honored that You chose my bed and my manger to serve Your needs. Stay as long as You wish and sleep in peace while I stand guard.*

Holly shook herself out of the memory. She leaned her head against the door frame and crossed her arms around herself. How much more of this could she take? At least the stupid angel had remained silent as she'd taken him from the kiln and shoved the cow inside. Silent, but there'd been a smirk on his face that hadn't been there this morning.

The memory of that satisfied smile raised prickly goose bumps on Holly's arms. Agitation crawled across her skin like a colony of tiny ants.

A car door slammed in the driveway, and Holly bolted out the house before Riley even made it to the porch. On the edge of the top step, she forced herself to stop and take a breath. If Riley noticed her anxiety, he'd want to know what was going on. She could only imagine the look on his face if she told him that his Nativity set was haunting her every waking moment. She had to get ahold of herself, or the evening would be ruined before it started.

She put a smile on her face, hoped it looked less forced than it felt, and waited for Riley to reach her. His answering grin took her breath away, and she welcomed the flutter of heat that started somewhere in her middle and bloomed to a blush that warmed her face. Her resolve strengthened. She needed the money this project would bring, and she wanted a chance to know Riley better, to see if the attraction she felt ran both ways. Flaking out on him over some imaginary voices in her head was a surefire way to ruin that.

Riley came up the short walk, schooling his steps to a leisurely stroll. The grin on his face probably hit to the far right of sappy. He couldn't help it. He'd thought Holly beautiful in yesterday's torn jeans and stained T-shirt. There weren't words in his vocabulary for how she looked tonight. The tiny breeze that stirred his hair played with the hem of her skirt, sending it dancing around a very attractive pair of legs. His gaze traveled upward, taking in the light teal sweater that outlined some incredibly sexy curves before finally landing on her face. Yesterday's smudge of dirt was long gone, and he could tell she'd spent some time on hair and makeup.

As unnecessary as that might be in Holly's case, a smart man recognized the effort and gave it its due.

When he reached the porch, he held out his hand. When Holly took it, he guided her down the steps. Once she was even with him, he lifted her hand over her head and motioned her into a quick spin. She complied. When she'd come around, her breath came out in an enchanting little giggle.

Riley placed his free hand over his heart. "Have mercy, but you're a sight."

Holly ducked her head, but not before he saw her satisfied smile. Riley pulled her hand through the bend of his arm and turned her toward his used Chevy Malibu. "Your chariot awaits." He led her to the passenger door and reached for the handle. Caution made him hesitate. He'd left all the windows open this afternoon while he'd worked on Ember's project. In spite of that and other precautions, he worried that Gilbert's fragrance lingered.

Instead of opening the car, he turned his back to it and leaned against the door. "Um, I should probably tell you that I had a little incident at work earlier."

Holly tilted her head. "Oh?"

"Yeah. Something that left the inside of my car a little...a lot"—he corrected ruefully—"smelly. I tried everything I could think of to fix that. Problem is, I think my olfactory senses have been permanently impaired. I can't smell anything, good or bad, at this point."

"Hmm." Holly motioned him aside, pulled open the door, and leaned in. She straightened so fast that she bumped her head on the door frame. "Oh, my goodness!"

Riley grabbed her around the waist in an effort to steady her as she whirled away from him and the car. "I'm sorry. I hoped it would be better by now." Were her shoulders shaking? Was she crying? "Oh man. Some date I turned out to be." He reached to feel for a bump on the back of her head. "Does it really hurt?" She flinched away from him and bent double. "Oh, Holly, I'm sorry. I..." His words trailed off as her gasping laughter reached him.

Holly turned to face him, hands pressed against her mouth and nose while tears ran down her face. "I'm not hurt, you goof. I'm choking."

The laughter in her words drove Riley back a step.

"I don't know what you hauled in there today, but"—she waved a hand in front of her face—"right now, it smells like a perfume factory exploded. What have you got in there?"

Riley shrugged. "I bought some piña colada vent clips and one of those green pine tree thingys for the rear-view mirror."

"And...?"

This time it was Riley's turn to duck his head. "Pretty much a whole bottle of lilac scented fabric freshener that I found under Mom's kitchen sink. Too much?"

"I'm surprised you didn't pass out on the way over here."

"I did feel a little lightheaded. I thought it was the anticipation of seeing you again."

Holly just chuckled. She opened the small purse that hung from her shoulder, extracted a set of keys, and jiggled them in front of him. "I'm driving. You need to leave that thing"—her finger jabbed the air in the direction of his car—"in the driveway with all four windows down. Maybe by the time we get back, you'll be able to drive home without asphyxiating yourself."

Holly followed Riley's instructions and made the turn onto the highway that connected Cable to Garfield and points beyond. "Where are we going?"

"Do you like Mexican type food?"

She slowed down for a light and glanced in his direction. "Mexican *type*?"

Riley shifted so that he faced her more directly. "Yeah. There's a new place out by the mall. They advertise Cuban food. I looked at their menu online, and most of what I saw looked like Mexican.

There might be a few different spices involved, but I'm game if you are. I've heard good things about it."

The light turned green, and Holly faced the road. "Sounds good. So...are you going to tell me?"

"Tell you what?"

"What construction materials you hauled in your car that called for such drastic cleaning methods."

"Construction materials?"

"You said it happened at work. You work for Dane, right?"

"Oh...what I do with Dad is just a part-time gig. I'm the new outreach pastor for Calvary Worship Church. I'm running the food bank over in Ashton."

Holly focused on her driving. Her outward "that's cool" didn't begin to express her feelings. A pastor and head of the food bank? Neither of those won him any points in her book. That he was a pastor meant he would likely try to shove religion down her throat. Between Sage and that stupid angel, she was getting all of that she needed, thank you very much. That he ran the food bank...

She shuddered as memories assailed her. Her well-defined sense of self-preservation slammed the door on those thoughts before they could take on a life of their own. She had no plans to go there with Riley or anyone else.

She must have hidden her feelings well because Riley continued. "So it wasn't a *what*. It was a *who*. I was actually going to ask you about it. Do you know someone named Gilbert Hoffman?"

Gilbert Hoffman.

Dad?

Holly's vision clouded, and her foot hit the brake before she'd had a conscious thought. In her peripheral vision, she saw Riley grabbing for a handhold as the car decelerated.

"Holly?"

Luckily there wasn't another car behind them. Holly struggled to breathe past the emotions that clogged her throat while she looked for a place to safely pull to the side of the road. An old, abandoned gas station appeared on her right, and she made the turn into the pothole-ridden drive. Her hands shook as she put the Jeep into park and leaned her head against the steering wheel. She heard Riley's seatbelt unlatch and shrugged away from the hand he laid on her shoulder.

"What's wrong? Are you sick?"

The sound that came from Holly's throat was neither affirmation or denial. She pulled in a shaky breath. "Give me a second." After a handful of deep breaths, she raised her head and faced Riley. "Gilbert Hoffman?"

"Do you know him?"

She shrugged, couldn't make herself form words.

Beside her, Riley shifted, but he didn't reach out again. "He came to the food bank today. He was in pretty bad shape. Says he lives with his wife, Cindy."

Gilbert...and Cindy. "Tell me what happened."

Riley told her the story while she stared numbly out the windshield. Of all the things she'd anticipated for this evening, having her deadbeat parents make an appearance hadn't been anywhere on the list.

When he finished, he paused a moment before prompting her. "Holly."

She chanced a glance in his direction.

"Do you know him?"

"Yeah." Holly faced him and licked her dry lips. "He's my dad. Cindy is my mom. And you, my friend, were taken in by the biggest con artist your little center is ever likely to see."

~

Riley took a few seconds to digest her words. Her parents? A con? "Why would you say that?"

"Because I lived it for most of my childhood." She bowed her head. "My parents had a lifetime membership at every food pantry in a hundred-mile radius when we were kids. Once their drug habits ate up any meager paychecks they might have had coming, my sister and I lived on the charities they could con food or money out of. Food banks, churches, thrift stores, the leftovers from neighborhood garage sales." Holly swallowed. "People like my parents are parasites, and centers like yours..." Her voice broke, and he heard tears in the words. "All you did for them was provide a safety net for their laziness and waste."

Her words knocked the breath out of him. How could she say such horrible things about a service that she admitted she'd benefited from? "That's a pretty harsh assessment."

"I can see why you'd think that. But, unless you spent a good part of your childhood being paraded around..." She stopped abruptly and bowed her head. "Never mind. It's ancient history."

"Maybe so. But have you ever thought about what might have happened without that *safety net*?"

She lifted her tear-stained face to his. "Yeah, lots of times. I wondered if my parents would have given Sage and me a real home if they'd been forced to rely on themselves."

"That's a pretty sad perspective. The man I saw today didn't appear to have the mental capacity to fend for himself."

Her eyes hardened. "What you saw was the result of years of bad choices, assuming it wasn't just an act." She sat back and crossed her arms. "What if I told you Gilbert had a business degree? A degree that should have gotten him a good job, a job that could have provided for his family. Instead, that degree is wasted and unused." She snorted. "He's got so many chemicals floating around his system, he probably doesn't even remember he has it." She jabbed a thumb into her chest. "I didn't have the benefit of college, but I run a house-cleaning service. I walk dogs. I sell cosmetics, and I craft. I'm saving money for a new car so I can drive Ubers. I'm living proof that you can make it in this world without that net if you want to. People like you—organizations like yours—take away the *want to.* I can promise that whatever good you tried to do for them today was wasted effort." She stopped to take a deep breath, holding up a hand when he opened his mouth to refute her words.

When she spoke again, her words carried a weariness that didn't suit her age. "Riley, I'm not stupid or blind, and I'm not heartless. I know you provide a valuable service for a lot of people. My parents are exceptions to the rule. At least I hope they are. But until there's a way to separate the genuinely needy from the eternally greedy, I can't support what you do. If I asked you to have nothing further to do with my parents, what would you say?"

Riley studied her face, his heart in his throat. She wasn't going to like his answer. "I'd have to ignore your request. We're here to help people, not judge them. The man I met today needed help, I was pleased to offer it. Not only is it my job, it's my Christian duty."

Holly nodded. "I figured as much." She put the car in gear, turned around, and took the road back the way they'd come.

"Where are we going now?"

"Home. I've lost my appetite."

"Holly, none of this means that we can't be friends."

She kept her eyes on the road, her words barely a whisper over the road noise. "Yeah, it does."

CHAPTER SEVEN

Holly didn't even wait for Riley to get out of the Jeep. As soon as the car was parked, she turned off the ignition, slammed out of the vehicle, and raced up the walk. If she gave herself time to think about it, she might have regretted her actions. She might have mourned the loss of a budding friendship. She might have taken time to apologize for her uncharacteristic rudeness.

But right now, those things were secondary to her need to talk with Sage. She'd find a solidarity with her sister that Riley would never understand.

She threw the door open and plowed into the house, stopping short when Sage looked up from her place on the sofa and the book she was reading. Her sister's eyes were wide and startled, and a hand covered her heart.

"Oh, you scared me to death!"

"They're back." Holly's voice was a cracked whisper.

Sage obviously needed no explanation. Her lips compressed into a thin line as she laid the book aside. She held out a hand to Holly, and when Holly took it, Sage pulled her down next to her. "Are you sure?"

Holly swallowed and tried to put her tangled thoughts in order.

It had been eight years since she'd seen her parents. And as harsh as it would sound to say, they'd been the most peaceful years of her life, and certainly the most secure. She took a deep breath. "They're in Ashton."

Sage studied Holly with an expression that Holly could only label as fear. Her voice shook when she asked, "You know this how?"

"Riley saw Dad today." Holly recounted Riley's story. By the time she finished, there were tears in both their eyes. "It's going to start all over again."

Sage wrapped her in a hug. "No, it won't. We aren't children anymore. They can't hurt us." She paused and Holly felt a shudder go through her sister's body. "They can't take advantage of us unless we allow it." She bowed her head and fell silent. After a few breaths, she said, "I won't ever allow him to take advantage of me again."

"Him?"

Sage straightened out of the hug. "Them. I meant them." She bowed her head, still holding Holly's hand. Holly heard a whispered "Jesus" and knew her sister was praying. She sat quietly, unsure what good prayer would do but unwilling to interrupt if it brought Sage a bit of peace.

While Sage sought solace in prayer, Holly mulled her own thoughts. As horrified as she was that Gilbert and Cindy were back, she was more angry than anything else. Her parents—and she used the word loosely—had managed to ruin every good thing in her life. Now, without even trying, they had come between her and Riley.

Riley had treated her with an easy affection Holly wasn't used to. Now, knowing who and what her parents were, he'd never look at her in the same way. It wasn't fair.

Honestly, it was embarrassing. Of all the emotions his revelation had brought, that was the surprising one.

She'd thought she'd gotten over the shame of them years before, but there it was, as real as the feel of her sister's soft hand against her palm.

Sage finally drew in a deep breath and raised her head.

What in the...? In the time it had taken to say a prayer, Sage's expression had morphed from a tangible fear to an eerie calm.

"You know," Sage began. "We might be blowing this out of proportion. We aren't the same people we were eight years ago. Maybe they've changed as well."

Holly scooted away a few inches. Who was this person who occupied her sister's body, and what had God done with the Sage who'd always had her back where Gilbert and Cindy were concerned? She'd bet money that the next word's out of Sage's mouth would be about her newfound religion and the prayer she'd just uttered.

"How can you say that?" Holly snapped. "Didn't you hear what I said? They're still looking for a handout wherever they can find one."

Sage took a deep breath before she spoke. "All I'm saying is that we shouldn't jump to conclusions. Maybe we should check out the situation for ourselves."

"Have you lost your mind? If they find out where we are, we won't have a moment's peace."

"They are our parents." Sage looked away and picked up the discarded book that lay on the sofa at her side. She stroked the leather cover. "The Bible—"

"I knew it! I knew you were going to drag your religion into this." Holly shoved up from the couch and paced a few steps away. "You and Riley," she muttered with a dismal chuckle.

"Me and Riley what?"

Holly shook her head, searching for the words to explain her feelings. Her love for Sage was immeasurable. Sage had been her rock when the people Holly should have been able to depend on failed in every way imaginable. Hurting her sister was the last thing she wanted, but some things needed to be said. She jabbed a finger at the book Sage held so reverently. "Do rose-colored glasses come as standard issue with that thing?"

Sage let the Bible lie in her lap while she titled her head. Her raised brows invited Holly to explain.

"When I tried to tell Riley how I felt about the situation, I hit the brick wall of his *Christian duty*." The last two words contained more than a hint of sneer. "So, I come home to you, my sister, who lived the same hell I did. My sister, who made a pact with me, a pact, I might add, that is for our parents' ultimate good, and you hold the Bible up as an excuse to excuse the inexcusable." She gathered her hair into a bundle at the nape of her neck and exhaled heavily, trying to see things from Sage's point of view.

"I get it, OK?" Holly said. "I get it that you've found something that gives you comfort. Something that you feel like you can depend on. We had precious little of that growing up. You're more than entitled. I'm happy for you even if I don't share it." She sat back down and looked Sage in the eye. "But those people are dangerous, and we don't owe them a single thing."

Sage stared off into the distance for a few seconds before she spoke. "Can I read something to you? It's part of our Sunday school lesson for tomorrow."

Holly sat back. She didn't like the look on Sage's face, didn't like the feeling that she'd lost this argument the moment Sage had picked up her Bible. "I guess."

Sage opened the book, muttering under her breath as she flipped through the delicate, gilded pages. "Corinthians...Galatians...Ephesians...here we are. Ephesians chapter four, verse thirty-two. 'And be ye kind one to another, tenderhearted, forgiving one another, even as God for Christ's sake hath forgiven you.'" She closed the Bible and laid it back in her lap. "I know you don't understand. I've been trying to explain it to you for weeks, and I guess I'm not doing a very good job. When I accepted Christ into my life, He forgave me for every bad thing I'd ever done." Her tear-filled eyes held Holly's as she crossed her arms over her middle and bent forward. "Every. Bad. Thing. Things I can't even forgive myself for...gone." She snapped her fingers. "Removed as far as the east is from the west. Pastor Hunter says that the reason that's important is that you can never travel so far east or west that you reach the end. That kind of unlimited forgiveness is the whole reason Christ was born."

Holly flinched when Sage's words began to echo Gabriel's.

Sage continued. "God forgave me for a lot of stuff. I guess I feel like I should return the favor."

Holly snorted and opened her mouth to speak, but Sage held up a hand.

"I'm not saying that I'm going to make Gilbert and Cindy a part of my life again. That ship sailed years ago, and I don't think that forgiveness equals gullibility. I just think, now that they're close by, maybe it would be OK to check on them. Maybe let them know that we don't hold a grudge."

No grudge? Holly had enough *grudge* to fill the Grand Canyon. She got up. "You do what you gotta do. Just leave me out of it. You're an adult. But I have a really bad feeling about this. If you aren't careful, that religion of yours is going to get you into a lot of trouble.

TWO-THIRTY A.M.

Holly threw the covers aside and sat on the edge of the bed. Watching the clock as the hours clicked by wasn't getting her anywhere but frustrated. She combed her fingers through her tangled curls. A major cause of her sleepless night was the argument with Sage. A small part was guilt at the way she'd treated Riley. He was wrong, but there might have been a better way to handle it. Most of what kept her awake were the haunted memories of a childhood she longed to forget and thoughts of the chaos that would rain into their lives if Gilbert and Cindy Hoffman were allowed back in. That was how she thought of them mostly. Gilbert and Cindy. Not Mom and Dad. They'd never earned those titles.

She slid off the side of the mattress. Trying to sleep was obviously pointless. If she didn't find something productive to do, the what-ifs were going to drive her crazy. With quiet motions, she opened her bedroom door and looked across the hall at the closed door that guarded Sage's private domain. An apology would get at least one thing off her mental plate. Maybe that would be enough to coax the sandman to sprinkle Holly with his magic sleepy dust.

She paused outside Sage's room. No sound or light filtered through the door, no indication that Sage suffered from any of the same regrets she did.

Maybe the righteous just sleep better.

Holly fisted her hands in her hair and rocked her head from side to side. That sort of snarky attitude would get her exactly nowhere.

She could get a couple of hours' work in on the Nativity set. She'd even risk the angel if it got her mind off everything that was keeping her awake. She made her way to the garage.

Thinking that the cow might be the lesser of the evils, since that story had to be pretty much complete, Holly opened the dormant kiln and withdrew the porcelain bovine. She held it under the light and examined the work she'd completed earlier in the afternoon. It looked good so far. The first coat of brown paint would serve as a base for accents of other colors. Beige for horns, the shaggy shock of hair between them, and the hoofs. Black for the eyes, lashes, and nose. White for the stockings and a few patches along her sides.

Holly set the cow on the worktable and opened the black paint. She'd work on the facial features and experiment with a few delicate strokes to add some contour where the limbs curled beneath the animal. The garage was blessedly quiet as she got started.

With her lips in a firm line of concentration, Holly began to paint the long lashes that would define the cow's eyes. She'd always admired the lashes on a newborn calf. Clover might not be a baby, but there was no rulebook that said she couldn't be pretty.

Thank you.

The words zipped through Holly's mind, quietly and non-threatening. She smiled in response. "You're welcome. When I get through with you, you'll be the envy of the barnyard.

"Could you paint the tuft of hair at the end of my tail black?"

Holly sat back and stared at Clover. *So much for cows not talking.* Oh well, for tonight, it beat solitude and the company of her own thoughts. "Black, really? I was thinking beige to match the hair between your horns."

"There's an old heifer's tale about black being the best for shooing flies."

Holly chuckled low in her throat. "Let me think about it while I finish this." The garage fell silent again as Holly drew in the last delicately upswept lash.

"Don't you think you were a little harsh?"

Gabriel's unexpected question startled Holly, and the brush skittered across the top of Clover's head, leaving a black line bisecting the space between her horns. Holly uttered a word she rarely used, reached for a cotton swab and the turpentine, and sent the angel a glare that would have intimidated a mere mortal. "You've got to stop doing that!" Holly cleaned up the mess, examined her handiwork, and then put the cow back in the kiln. Once her paints were put away, she crossed her arms over her chest and addressed the angel. "How was I harsh? I told her I'd think about the black on her tail."

Gabriel mirrored her pose. "Not with Clover. You can paint the end of her tail purple for all I care. With Riley and your sister."

Holly tilted her head. "How do you...?" Her words trailed off as she studied the angel. Neither of those arguments had happened anywhere near the garage. "I thought you couldn't read my mind."

"I can't, but the Father keeps me updated when I'm on assignment." He produced a scroll from midair and shook it open. "Stubbornness, unforgiveness, anger." He peered at her over the scroll, and she actually heard him sigh. "You really need to work on those things."

Holly found herself doing a mental count to ten. Her movements were jerky as she rolled her chair back to the edge of the table, sat, and leaned over the angel. "If your *Father* keeps you so well informed, maybe you should ask Him why I feel the way I do. In the meantime, maybe you should mind your own business and stick to the Christmas story. At least that's a topic you might understand."

"I understand only what the Father tells me. The Father understands all things. He'd help you if you'd allow Him to."

The angel's words were too much. How was she supposed to work with this sort of distraction? Holly looked over the collection of figurines as a sudden certainty struck her. She rose from her place at the table, crossed to a shelving unit, and returned with a stack of boxes. After opening one, she reached for the donkey.

"What are you doing?" Gabriel asked.

Her voice was resigned when she answered. "Packing this away. After the way I treated Riley tonight, there's no way he's gonna pay me to complete the project." Donkey nestled in paper cushioning, she set the box aside, opened another, and reached for the baby in the manger. As soon as her hands closed around it, words filled her head.

I love you. I came to earth just for you.

Holly shook her head clear and finished packing the boxes. She reached for the angel last.

"You're making a mistake."

Holly nestled him into the shredded paper. "I don't think so. If there's no money in it for me, then you guys are wasting my time. Maybe I'll get back to you next year. Hopefully by then, you'll have found someone else to haunt." She lowered the lid, doing her best to ignore the chorus of protests that crowded her mind. One voice rang above the others as she left the garage.

I love you. I came to earth just for you.

She paused at the door that led back into the house and looked over her shoulder at the stack of boxes. Part of her wished she could bring herself to believe that.

CHAPTER EIGHT

When Holly parked outside Crafted with Love on Monday morning for their weekly meeting, her eyes were gritty from lack of sleep. She was tired and out of sorts. She'd spent her Sunday breathing the same air as Sage but having no real interaction with her. Numerous times an apology hovered on her lips, but the words never seemed to make it past the lump in her throat.

She entered the back room of the shop, freshened her ever-present cup of coffee, cut a humongous apple fritter in half, and took a seat on the far side of the room. If she sat on the fringe of activity and spoke only when spoken to, maybe she could get on with her day.

Sounds like a plan.

With her scheduling app open on her phone, she scrolled through the day's obligations. The Harris house had to be cleaned before lunch. She'd intentionally scheduled them for Monday morning, since they were a retired couple with no kids. Their house was an easy way to start the week and wouldn't take more than a couple of hours. Cleaning the Cox house would occupy most of her afternoon. The final job on her Monday schedule was a trip to Pet Rite to pick up the Greenbaum's two adorable Labradoodles from the groomers. After she dropped the dogs off at home, Holly would be free to head home to tend to the Avon order that had to be turned in. That meant spending a couple of hours on the phone, trying to catch up with straggling customers. No one could accuse her of being a slacker.

Holly broke off a piece of the fritter. It was barely eight in the morning, and she was already looking forward to the end of the day. At least she didn't have to work on the Nativity set tonight. As much as she was going to miss the boost to her income, she wasn't too upset to have that project off her plate.

She pulled another piece of the pastry free and glanced at Sage from under her lowered lashes. Her sister was seated across the room, engrossed in a whispered conversation with Piper Goodson. Sage was giving the fritters a wide berth, but Piper, seven-plus months pregnant and about to burst, was nearly licking her paper plate clean of crumbs.

Holly caught the words *amazing sermon* and knew they were discussing their church services from yesterday. She studied her sister. How could Sage look so content with the unresolved differences between them? The issue of their parents crouched in the background like a mythical boogie man that only Holly could see. The only myth was Sage's misguided belief that reaching out to Gilbert and Cindy could produce anything but more heartache. Holly swallowed, forcing the bite of fritter past the obstruction in her throat. She hated being at odds with her sister. You couldn't live in the same house with someone and not have an occasional argument, no matter how much you loved her. But more than a day of tiptoeing around each other was almost unprecedented. Before they went their separate ways for the day, she had to try and make that right.

"What's wrong?"

Holly looked up, startled out of her thoughts by Maggie's question. "Hmm?"

Maggie tossed her long black hair over a shoulder and gave

Holly a friendly smile. "You don't look like you. I know it's Monday morning, but is it really that bad?"

The torture of being raised by Gilbert and Cindy Hoffman was enough to sour anyone's day but it wasn't anything Holly planned to share. She sipped at her coffee before she replied. "Just a case of the blahs." In a bid to change the subject, Holly clasped Maggie's hand and brought her arm up to eye level. A series of beaded bracelets, some delicate, others chunky, all sparkly, encircled her wrist.

"Those are pretty. Your work?" Holly studied the young home-health aide. "Won't those get in the way of caring for your patients?"

Maggie's smile widened. "Yeah, if I planned to wear them out of the store." Reaching into the pockets of her bright yellow scrubs, she pulled out a double handful of her colorful creations and dumped them on the table. Beads in every shape and color glinted in the light. "The kids went out of town with their foster father this weekend. Since we're gearing up for Christmas, I spent my free time making these. Bracelets don't take any time to put together, and they make great, inexpensive stocking stuffers." She raked the bracelets off her wrist and added them to the pile.

Holly's eyes landed on a creation interspersed with fat purple and crystal stones. She sent her sister another glance. The beads of Sage's earrings were almost a perfect match, just smaller, almost as if they'd been made by the same crafter. That was a distinct possibility considering the ladies' penchant for sampling each other's wares.

Holly and Sage both had a few of Maggie's creations in their jewelry boxes. But their sampling went beyond shiny trinkets. One of Ember's fall wreaths hung on their front door, Holly slept under one of Lacy's quilts, and a couple of Ruthie's rustic signs decorated their kitchen. Holly'd also noticed the addition of one of Piper's crosses hanging over Sage's bed. The other women were just as enamored with Sage's soaps and candles and Holly's ornaments. With such easy access to so many beautiful items, it was a constant battle not to be each other's best customers. That certainly wasn't going to change today. The purple bracelet was the perfect peace offering. Holly slid it free. "How much for this one?"

"You can have it if you like it."

Holly shook her head. She knew Maggie was saving for a specific goal just as much as Holly was. Holly wanted a new car, but Maggie was saving for something even more important—a bigger apartment for when she got her kids back. "Not a chance. How much were you planning to sell them for?"

Maggie blew out a frustrated breath. "Just once I'd like one of you guys to accept a gift." She picked up the bracelet and bounced it in her palm as if weighing it. "Can we at least do my cost?"

"That works."

"Five dollars."

"Sold." Holly pulled a wad of bills out of her jeans pocket and counted out five ones. "Thanks." She slipped the beaded circle onto her own wrist as Ember entered the room.

Holly would catch Sage after the meeting.

Ember took a few seconds to fix her own cup of coffee before she faced the gathered crafters. "Ladies, I know everyone has a busy day ahead, so let's get started." Ember paused and looked down at her phone. When she raised her head, she had a happy smile on her face. "I am pleased to report that the storage area in the basement is filling up with Christmas stock. We are not going to be caught short this year. You guys don't know how much I appreciate your efforts." She focused her attention on the older woman seated nearest to her. "Ruthie, let's start with you. What are you working on?"

Smile lines crinkled at the corners of Ruthie's blue eyes. "Oh, a little bit of this and a little bit of that. I went to an estate sale over the weekend. I found a couple of old, beat-up nightstands that will be perfect washbasin stands once I get them refinished. And I saw an idea in a magazine I'd like to try if I can find an old wooden door or two." She made motions with her hands. "Distress them, refinish them, cut them in half, and put the pieces together at right angles. Then I'll add two or three small shelves. Lovely corner pieces."

Lacy leaned forward. "Oh, I want one for my kitchen."

Ruthie's gray head shook as she laughed at Lacy's eagerness, but it was Ember who spoke.

"I love it. I'll ask Dane to keep his eye out for some doors if you want."

"Thanks. I want, but I gotta warn you, some of this stuff will take up more space than you're used to me using."

"You'll have all the space you need," Ember assured her before turning to Lacy. "How about you?"

Lacy Fields licked fritter glaze from her fingers. "My sewing machine is humming day and night. We'll have plenty of quilts."

Ember nodded. "Good. I'm loving the holiday table sets. I predict that the runners, placemats, and matching napkins are going to be a hot item this year." She rubbed her hands together and looked at Piper Goodson.

"You poor thing, you look like you're about to pop. How are you doing?"

Piper sat back in her chair and rubbed her enormous belly. "I'm...we're fine. I'd be lying if I said this little bundle of joy wasn't sucking all my energy, but the good news is that most of what I do, I can do sitting down, plus I started my maternity leave last Friday. I have a couple of crosses completed and stacked in the spare bedroom. I just haven't had the get-up-and-go to deal with them. I'll have Evan load them up and haul them over here sometime this week." Piper looked at Holly. "I wanted to do a few with Christmas themes. I saw your display of small ceramic bells and snowflakes. I may try and incorporate some of those."

"Help yourself. Just keep track of what you use. I'll cut you a deal."

Ember's gaze skimmed across Holly and landed on Sage. "I know you are working on a lot of projects. The shop never smelled better. Your soaps and candles are practically walking out of the store. Any progress on the hand creams and scrubs?"

Holly felt a surge of pride for her sister as Sage smiled. "Success. We'll have those items on the shelf next week in five fragrances. I'm just waiting on the packaging I ordered. In the meantime..." She bent down and pulled a plastic sack from her enormous bag, opened it, and set a collection of sealed, plastic condiment cups on the table. "I brought samples of the hand cream for all of you to try." She opened one as the ladies gathered around to claim their freebies and sniffed. "This is the orange Dreamsicle and my personal favorite," Sage said. "I love the burst of citrus combined with a soft hint of vanilla. The other scents I've perfected are birthday cake, apple pie, strawberries and cream, and piña colada. If I don't already have candles and soaps in those fragrances, I will by next month." She looked at Ember. "I was thinking of putting a few gift baskets together as a trial, if you think they'll sell."

Ember peeled the lid off her sample and took a deep breath. Her eyes drifted closed in appreciation. "Oh, they'll sell. I have no doubt about that."

The women settled back into their places. There was a lull in the discussion while each of the women gave Sage's hand cream a try.

"I love the smell," Lacy said.

Maggie's eyes closed in delight. "The texture is just amazing."

"My hands needed this." Ruthie sighed as she rubbed the cream in. "The stains and the paints make them so dry. I think I need to order a tub of this right up front."

Sage beamed, and Holly reveled in her sister's success. It had always been that way. A win for one was a win for both. She twisted the bracelet, more eager than before for the meeting to be over, for the breach in their relationship to be healed.

Ember took back control of the meeting. "Holly, you showed me what you were working on when you stopped by on Friday. Anything else to add?"

Holly shook her head and looked at her sister. "Anything I said at this point would be anticlimactic."

"OK, just one more thing. Construction of the new shelves should begin in a few days. I've been assured that they will try and keep the mess to a minimum. If you have any specific ideas about products you think we should stock, now's the time to share." Ember looked around with a gigantic smile. "We are going to be *the* place for Garfield holiday shopping. I am beyond proud of each and every one of you." She waved a hand at the door. "You guys go and have a great day."

Holly hung back for a few seconds as everyone shifted. Some went to talk with Ember while others huddled around the fritters and coffee, getting their final hit of sugar and caffeine to aid them on their Monday morning journey.

Holly took up a position next to the door as the familiar notes of Sage's ring tone sounded.

Sage propped her bag in a chair while she dug for the phone with both hands. "Sage Hoffman."

Holly saw a frown gather between her sister's delicate brows as Sage removed the bag from the seat and sank into it herself. "You're kidding. We told them eggshell, didn't we?"

Holly leaned against the wall. She didn't want to eavesdrop on her sister's business, and from this vantage point she wouldn't miss her. With a deliberate effort, she redirected her attention and tuned into the not-so-private conversation happening between Ember and Ruthie. She caught the words *after Christmas* and *craft classes*.

What a fun idea. Holly would need to be sure to add her positive vote to that suggestion. Movement drew her attention back to Sage as her sister started for the door with the phone pressed to her ear. Holly took off the bracelet and held out a hand to stop Sage. Even if there wasn't time for the words that needed to be said, Sage wouldn't mistake the bracelet for anything other than an apology.

"You tell them not to paint another inch. I'll be there in five minutes."

Sage brushed past Holly and her peace offering without a

glance and sailed through the door. It closed behind her with a sharp snap.

Holly stood rooted to the spot, dumbfounded. She clasped her hands around the bracelet and bowed her head. Stung by Sage's rejection, there was no way to stem the tears that sprang into her eyes.

CHAPTER NINE

There were a gazillion reasons to explain Sage's abrupt exit that had nothing to do with their weekend disagreement, but in that split second, her sister's motivation didn't matter. All that mattered was the tsunami of emotions that slammed into Holly's heart like debris from an Oklahoma tornado. The fallout from that wind rained down around Holly in a blanket of misery.

The rift between her and Sage. The disquiet generated by the return of her parents. The surreal interaction with the Nativity set and her secret fear that she was losing her grip on reality. On top of all that, the regret over her treatment of Riley and the fact that she'd torpedoed any chance of getting to know him better. Everything crashed in on her at once. Overwhelmed her.

There wasn't a force on this earth, much less inside Holly, that could have prevented the sob of despair that nearly crumpled her as she stood looking at the door that had slammed shut in her face.

Ruthie was by her side in an instant. The older woman's arm came around Holly's shoulders and drew her in close. Swept away by the comfort and support Ruthie's touch provided, Holly let the tears fall.

Ruthie's arms tightened. One hand pressed Holly's head

against her shoulder while she smoothed her hair with the other. "Sweetheart, what's wrong? Are you sick? Are you in pain?"

Holly managed to shake her head. Ruthie's touch generated a feeling of security that was almost forgotten, something Holly hadn't experienced in nearly two decades. Something cracked loose inside her as she dredged up the name that went with the feeling. *Motherly.*

Holly sank against the older woman. She hadn't been mothered since...the memory that twisted her heart was too painful to dwell on. She hadn't been mothered in way too long. The thought brought on a fresh batch of tears. Sage had always been the one to hold her when she cried. The one to comfort her when the world was scary. As much as she loved her sister, as dependable as Sage's presence had always been, what Ruthie offered was something different, something longed for in the dead of night, something that filled the empty spots in her heart. Instead of abating, the tears turned from sorrowful to ugly.

Ruthie's arms slackened, and Holly clung tighter, hesitant to forfeit the connection. *You're making a fool of yourself*, a little voice from somewhere deep inside whispered. Holly didn't care. Something inside her heart had been searching for this feeling for almost twenty years. She intended to hold onto it for just a while longer.

"It's OK," Ruthie whispered. "I've got you, and I'm not going anywhere. I just thought you might want to sit down."

Holly swallowed back the tears. "Yes."

"That's a girl. You just hang on and walk with me. We'll sit, and you can tell us what's got you in such a state."

Us?

Holly opened her eyes just wide enough to look over Ruthie's shoulder, and her heart sank. Ember, Maggie, Lacy, and Piper all stood there, wringing their hands, their expressions reflecting varying degrees of concern. Her eyes clenched shut. What had she done? What had she been thinking when she'd allowed the dam to burst?

Allowed?

There'd been no *allowing.*

As if sensing Holly's sudden awareness and the embarrassment that came with it, Ruthie whispered in Holly's ear. "Don't you worry. We all have moments when we need each other. We're all here for you, and we won't press. This is a safe space.

Holly let Ruthie lead her to the table. Ruthie settled her in a chair and took the seat beside her. She scooted the chair close as if sensing that Holly needed the extra few inches of moral support.

Piper, Lacy, and Maggie joined them at the table. Ember set a fresh mug of hot coffee in front of Holly and claimed one of the remaining chairs for herself.

Holly bent her head over the cup and breathed in the hot, fragrant steam. Despite her shattered emotions, something about the scene felt familiar. Holly groped for the memory, surprised when it surfaced. It had been on a day just like this, with them all gathered together, when Ember had shared the betrayal that had changed her life.

Holly bit her lip as she considered all the good that had come from that day. An acquaintance between seven women had been forge-welded into a friendship that morning, one that was still growing strong months later. Maybe Ruthie was right. This was a safe place.

"Holly?" Maggie reached across the table and pressed a tissue into Holly's hand. "Can you tell us what's wrong? We don't need to know any more or less than you're willing to share. There may not be anything we can do to fix it, but we can listen, and we can pray."

Holly's hand clutched around the tissue. She knew Maggie's offer was sincere, but she didn't believe in prayer. Hadn't she spent her childhood looking for, and failing to find, something...someone...to trust in? Hadn't that experience taught her that, except for Sage, the only person she could really trust in this world was herself? The thought brought a nudge of discomfort. How could she call these women her friends in one breath and withhold trust from them in the next?

You can't.

Holly sat up straight and mulled the words that had just landed in her consciousness. Her mind had rendered the thought in Gabriel's voice. That was impossible, though, right? That stupid angel was thirty miles away, closed in a box, locked in a garage.

You can't get rid of me that easily. I'm an angel, after all.

Holly closed her eyes, put her fingers to her temples, and rubbed.

"Do you have a headache?" Lacy reached for her purse. "I think I have some aspirin."

Holly shook her head. "No, I'm fine." When she opened her eyes, she could almost feel the love and concern that radiated off her friends. Other than those few unguarded moments with Riley, she'd never shared her childhood with anyone. Would they really understand?

She jerked her head toward the door. "Sorry about that. Sage and I got some upsetting news this weekend." Holly dropped the twisted tissue onto the table and smoothed it flat. It helped to have something other than their worried expressions to focus on. "Instead of dealing with it like adults, we...well, mostly me, argued about it."

"Oh, she'll get over it," Piper said. "My sister Madison and I argue all the time. Sometimes, I think it's what sisters do best. But you know what?"

Holly looked up in time to catch Piper twisting in the hard chair.

"We're sisters. Love always wins in the end."

"Thanks. I hope so," Holly whispered. That should be the end of it, right? A bout of tears, a flimsy explanation, reassurance offered, everyone goes about their day. She should be gathering her things and heading out the door. Instead it felt like her butt was glued to the chair. Suddenly the idea of unloading a lifetime of emotional baggage was the most important thing in her life.

And where was that coming from all of a sudden? Of herself and Sage, Holly was the more private. Heart-to-heart conversations with anyone other than Sage rarely happened. Fine, *never* happened. And even if she wanted to unload her heart on these women, this was just as much Sage's story as hers. Before she shared with friends, she needed Sage's permission. Didn't she?

So the conversation ended there, and all was well. Except that it wasn't. When Holly tried to stand the heaviness in her heart threatened to buckle her knees.

But what about Sage?

What about her? It wasn't as if there were some promise between them to keep their past private. Worrying about what Sage would think was just another effort on the part of her subconscious to get out of this room with her secrets intact. If the situation were reversed and Sage needed to talk it out, Holly would support that decision. Sage might be peeved at her right now, but confiding in these women would not make that worse.

Holly lifted the coffee mug to her mouth and swallowed a fortifying sip. "It's more than a simple disagreement. Our parents are back."

A collection of cocked heads and furrowed brows met her comment.

Ember leaned forward, her expression filled with compassion. "We're listening."

Those two simple words coated Holly's heart like a soothing balm and gave her the courage to continue. "Gilbert and Cindy Hoffman, the biological units that produced Sage and me, are parasites." Holly paused, knowing full well the effect her bitter words would have on her friends. She wasn't disappointed. The other women in the room glanced at each other and stirred uncomfortably in their seats.

Ruthie was the first to speak, her voice both accepting and encouraging. "That's...harsh." When Holly turned to face her, Ruthie met Holly's gaze with steady eyes and reclaimed her hand. "Since you aren't a harsh person, I have to believe that you have a good reason for the words."

Holly pulled in a deep breath and decided that the only way to get through what was to come was by keeping her attention focused on the motherly figure seated beside her. Something in Ruthie's calm presence soothed a hurt that had built and festered for years. "Thank you."

"For...?" Ruthie asked.

"For being you. For not being shocked or discounting my words without a fair hearing."

Ruthie simply squeezed Holly's hand, the gentle pressure urging her to continue her story.

Holly cleared her throat. "What would you say if I told you that I don't have a single memory of a family meal, a bedtime story, Christmas morning, or even a day at the park that included my parents?"

Ruthie frowned, and the compassion that filled her eyes had fresh tears bubbling up in Holly's. She blinked them back, forced her gaze away from Ruthie's, and focused on the calendar hanging on the wall over the older woman's right shoulder.

"I don't think Gilbert and Cindy ever intended to have a family. They certainly never intended to raise one, but birth control cost money, and abstinence requires focus. Their money was better spent on their latest addiction. Focus was always a victim of those addictions."

She brought her attention back to Ruthie. "We, Sage and I, would probably have been abandoned at birth if it hadn't been for our nana, Cindy's mother." Holly closed her eyes and felt a sad smile twitch the corners of her mouth. "Nana was the best, our lifeline. And even though she was seventy by the time I came along, she took care of us all by herself. She made sure we had hot meals, clean clothes, and a warm bed. On the rare occasion my parents showed up on her doorstep, high or broke or both, she did her best to shelter us from their neglect. She couldn't hide the fact that our parents didn't want us, but having her in our lives numbed the effect.

"She had a stroke when I was five. Sage had just turned seven. We found her when the bus dropped us off from school. She was already gone. Gilbert and Cindy were there, sleeping it off in the upstairs bedroom."

Tears filled Holly's eyes, tears she couldn't have held back at gunpoint. "I despise them for that. I've wondered my whole life what would have happened if they'd helped her, if the things that happened next would have been different."

Someone sniffed. Holly turned toward the sound. Lacy was dabbing her eyes with a napkin. When she saw Holly look in her direction, she pressed her lips together and drew in a shaky breath. "You poor babies. I know that there are people who turn their backs on their children. I'll never understand how people can take the most precious gift God ever gave them and not love them, not cherish them..." Her words faded as her expression grew fierce. "I would sacrifice the rest of my life for one more day with my Olivia." Lacy folded in on herself and covered her face with the damp napkin. "I'm sorry," she whispered. "This is not about me."

On her right, Maggie put an arm around Lacy's shoulders and whispered something. Lacy shook her head as her shoulders heaved in silent sobs.

Piper spoke, drawing Holly's attention away from Lacy. "What happened after your nana died?"

And there lay the crux of it all. A story no one knew except her and Sage. She looked around the room. Maggie still held the weeping Lacy, but that storm seemed to be ebbing. Piper watched Holly with a combination of curiosity and empathy. Ruthie still maintained her position next to Holly. She'd begun to rub Holly's back as the story bubbled forth. It should have been annoying but Holly found the contact comforting. Her gaze shifted to Ember. She leaned forward, eyes closed, her lips moving in what Holly figured was prayer. *As if that ever made a difference in anything.*

Holly's gaze went back to Piper. "What happened?" She drew in air, but it didn't feel like it was enough to inflate her lungs. She huffed it out and tried again, this time forcing the oxygen as deep as it would go. She exhaled the air with the truth. "Eleven years of hell."

CHAPTER TEN

Suddenly stifled by the closeness of her friends, Holly scooted away from the table and crossed to the small window over the sink.

She needed a moment.

The sight of the green dumpsters, the red brick wall across the alley, and a half dozen vehicles blurred into a mishmash of color as memories surfaced and feelings tugged her into a past she'd never intended to revisit, much less share.

Her phone vibrated in her pocket, and she pulled it out to look at the screen. The Harrises needed to reschedule. That was fine. She wasn't in the mood to hurry off to work just now anyway. Holly tapped in a quick message and put the phone away.

Someone shifted at the table behind her, the whisper of fabric on the plastic seat of the chair echoing in the quiet room. Holly closed her eyes. They were waiting on her to continue. She took a deep breath in through her nose and blew out through pursed lips before turning to lean against the counter and face her friends.

"Life changed for Sage and me that day. Nana filled a gap we hadn't known existed. Once she was gone, we got a hard lesson in living with addicts whose first thought in the morning and last thought at night wasn't caring for their daughters but what they had to do to get their next fix." Her shoulders slumped. "*Living with* might be too generous a term now that I think about it."

Lacy's eyes were clear of tears as she sat straight. "They abandoned you?"

"I wish it had been that straightforward," Holly said as she came back to the table and took her seat. "Sage and I would have been better off as wards of the state than in the not-so-loving care of our parents. As I said, Gilbert and Cindy never wanted us. Their idea of childcare was dumping us in Nana's lap and coming for a visit three or four times a year when they ran out of money. Once Nana was gone, they had no clue and didn't really want one."

Holly wrapped cold hands around her mug and bowed her head. She caught her reflection in the dark liquid and smirked. "They had no clue, but they had a network."

"What sort of network?" Piper asked.

Holly looked up, her gaze moving from one woman to the next. She figured she was about to ruffle some Christian feathers, but there was no way to tell the story and avoid that. "Sage and I called it the handout parade. It might have kept us alive, but we despised it."

She met the puzzled frowns of her friends with a sad smile. "We'll come back to that, I promise." Holly continued. "Nana's house was the only home we ever knew. It was a safe place for us. She never allowed our parents to stay for more than a few days at a time. Looking back, I figure she did that as much for herself as for us. They would have bled her dry if she'd allowed it.

"Once she was gone"—Holly swiped a tear from her cheek—"well, I guess she did what she thought was best for us."

"Why do I get the feeling that this is only going to get worse?" Maggie asked.

Holly ignored the question. "Nana left the house and what money she had tied up in legal red tape. The house went to Cindy and Gilbert, along with just enough money in a trust fund to allow her lawyer to keep the taxes and insurance paid under the condition that it was theirs as long as Sage and I lived there. There were also instructions that the house couldn't be sold before Sage turned eighteen. Nana didn't have a lot of money. Making sure we had a place to live after she was gone was all she could do. I was only five when she died, so I can't speak with any certainty about her reasoning, but It doesn't take a lot of imagination to guess that she hoped her daughter would eventually wake up and be a mother."

"I'm going to guess that never happened," Ember said.

"Not even for a day." Holly rose a second time and paced the small area between the sink and the table. "You know, I'm not going to say my parents didn't try, at least at first. I have some spotty memories of Gilbert leaving for work in the mornings and Cindy packing us a lunch and walking us to the bus stop. But a zebra can't change its stripes, and an addict is an addict is an addict. Most of my memories of the time between Nana's death and Sage's eighteenth birthday are layered in uncertainty. Wondering if there would be food in the fridge. Times when I could barely sit still in class because my feet ached in shoes that were too small. Days at a time when we didn't see either of our parents."

Ruthie sat back in her chair, disbelief on her face. "They left you alone?

Holly's chuckle lacked any nuance of humor. "More often than I care to remember. A night or two at a time, here and there, over the years. Then there was the rare occasion when one or both of them managed to get a job. Those times never lasted for long, but childcare wasn't in their budget while they worked. Why invite someone into your home who could report all your dirty laundry to the authorities? I'd say they were home about half the time, holed up in their room upstairs, zonked out of their minds on the latest drug of choice. It didn't take us long to learn that going up there to ask them for anything was a waste of time. When they were passed out, we couldn't have roused them if the house was on fire. If they were high, they were no help. We learned to be self-sufficient in a hurry." She returned to her seat and took a sip of her coffee to wet her throat.

Ember took advantage of the pause to refill her own cup. She held up the pot. "Anyone else?"

As the carafe was passed around the table, Holly noticed Lacy frowning at her.

"You have a question?" Holly asked. "Ask away. It's true confession time."

"I'm just...I guess..." Lacy held up her hands in frustration. "You're painting a picture I don't think any of us can really identify with. I believe every word you've said, but..." She stopped, and her mouth moved as she searched for her next words. "Your parents must have been spending a lot on their habit. You had no income, no supervision... I don't want to offend you, but how did you survive?"

Piper had questions of her own. She sat back, her arms crossed over her pregnant belly. "I'm not even supposed to eat lunch meat because of the additives they use in the processing. How did your mother use drugs through two pregnancies and not have children riddled with birth defects or any of the dozen issues that give me nightmares?"

Holly answered Piper's question first. "I've asked myself the pregnancy question a dozen times. I even googled it to try and understand how Sage and I managed to arrive as healthy, normal babies. From what I've read, all the bad things associated with drug use during pregnancy aren't written in stone. They *could* happen, they *might* happen"—she shrugged—"in our case, they didn't happen."

Ruthie put her elbows on the table and lowered her head into her hands. "'Before I formed thee in the belly, I knew thee...' God's grace," she whispered.

Holly bit her lip at the words. "Let's call it the luck of the draw and leave it at that." She turned her attention to Lacy. "How did we survive?" She answered the question with two words. "The network."

"What sort of network?" Ember asked. "Friends, family?"

"I wish." Holly crossed her arms and leaned back in her chair. "Food banks and churches mostly. Thrift stores, garage sales." When none of the women responded, she continued. "When Gilbert and Cindy couldn't find employers who weren't too picky about who they hired, or when their unemployment was exhausted between jobs, they had a plan that never failed to produce results. They had a list of food banks a mile long along with every church that had ever offered a handout, and they were fast learners. They figured out that people might be able to say no to two adults looking for another handout, but when you have two pitiful looking little girls tagging along, it's a lot harder. Every couple of months or so, they'd sober up enough to clean up, load Sage and me into the car, and make the rounds."

"The handout parade," Maggie said.

"Exactly. From churches to food banks to thrift stores. Always a story, always a con, always mortifying." Embarrassment bubbled up in her throat and lodged there like a hunk of unchewed meat. She was forced to stop and take a breath, to give the tears that threatened a chance to recede. "It was bad enough when we were small and didn't really understand what was happening. But I'll never forget the humiliation the first time I realized that the looks we were getting from people was pity and..." The story paused while she looked for the right word. "Disgust. Disgust at my parents. Pity for me and Sage and the fact that we were such obvious pawns in their game."

"You poor babies," Ruthie whispered.

Holly flinched away from the words she'd grown up hearing. Words that described her miserable childhood. "We managed." The remark was delivered in a deadpan tone. A defensive mechanism cultivated over the years. Her thoughts went back to her conversation with Riley Saturday night. He hadn't understood her position, and she wouldn't risk a second argument trying to explain it this morning. The whole food bank thing was her own personal soapbox. She knew that her reasoning, though valid for her situation, was difficult to understand and didn't apply to the system as a whole.

"As we got older, Sage and I figured out ways to earn a few dollars here and there."

"Doing what?" Maggie asked. "You were just children."

"Oh, you'd be surprised what a couple of enterprising young girls can accomplish when they need a new pair of tennis shoes." *Or if the electricity has been off for a day or two.* She didn't say the words aloud. "By the time Sage was twelve and I was ten, we were walking dogs for the whole neighborhood. There were several elderly couples on the surrounding blocks that had mowers but no energy to mow. We got paid to do their yard work. Thanks to leaves in the fall, snow shoveling in the winter, and spring and summer upkeep, some of those yards were year-round money-makers. We washed cars. There were babysitting gigs. We cleaned out garages. You name it, if it meant a little extra money in the kitty, if it put off the parade for a few days, we were up for it.

Ember smiled. "I'm so sorry you girls had to go through that, but it trained you well. That experience explains why you are both such go-getters today."

"I won't argue that," Holly said. "Things got a little better once Sage was old enough to open her own savings account. Once that happened, Gilbert and Cindy couldn't get to our stash anymore."

"Your parents stole from you?" Lacy's eyebrows arched in shock.

Holly's mirthless chuckle bounced off the walls. "That and they had a tidy little business selling the extra bounty from the food banks. Nothing was safe from them."

Maggie held up a hand. "They sold your food?"

"Yep. We always came back from the parade with more groceries than we could use, things Sage and I didn't know how to cook or things that our parents weren't about to take the time to mess with. They'd sort them out and put the extra in a separate refrigerator. Those groceries would then be traded for drugs or cigarettes...maybe even cash if they needed to pay a bill. They had a very productive little business on the side."

Maggie put her head in her hands.

"That's horrible," Lacy whispered.

"That's Gilbert and Cindy Hoffman," Holly said. "Anyway, Sage and I each had real jobs by the time we were fifteen. Once we did, we put our foot down on continuing the parades. We'd had all the humiliation we could stomach. A few days after Sage's eighteenth birthday, Mom and Dad went off on one of their little overnighters, and they never came back. Until now."

"You've seen them?" Ruthie asked.

"No, but Riley Soeurs has. Holly shared the relevant bits of Saturday night's conversation. "They were gone for eight blissful years. I have no idea what they want or even if trying to contact us is on their agenda, but the thought of seeing them again, the thought of having to deal with them again, scares me to death."

"And Sage doesn't feel the same way?" Maggie asked.

Holly studied her friend. Here came the Christian feather-ruffling. She braced for the backlash. "She feels like it's her *Christian* duty to reach out to them. I think she's out of her mind. These people took everything we ever had and destroyed it." Fury nearly choked her. "They slept while the only person who loved us died. They destroyed our childhood. The house that Nana left us? They trashed it so thoroughly that when they took off, we were forced to find a new place to live. Why would we want to open ourselves back up to their form of abuse? I'd be perfectly happy if they were dead and buried."

Ruthie's eyes widened in unmistakable shock. "Sweetheart, you don't mean that."

Holly shrugged, too wrung out to argue the point. "Anyway, Sage and I had a disagreement, one I'd hoped to make right, but she got away before I could." She fidgeted in her seat, twisting the beads of the purple bracelet. Now that the story was told, she knew what came next. An offer of prayer. As much as she loved these women, Holly just wasn't up for such a pointless exercise. She glanced at the clock near the door and found the perfect excuse to bring this show and tell to a timely close. The store opened in five minutes.

She pushed to her feet and nodded at the clock. "I love you guys, and I appreciate you giving me the time to vent, but I've kept you too long this morning. We should probably get busy." Holly looked at Ember. "My morning job canceled, so I've got some time. I'll go unlock the front door while you straighten up back here."

Once in the main part of the store, Holly headed for the door. She stopped abruptly when she saw Riley standing there with his face pressed against the glass like a little kid admiring the candy through the window. Her heart did a little stutter-dance. Was he looking for her? *Don't be silly. He's probably here to get started on the shelves.* Either way, as much as she liked him, as much as she'd hoped to see him again, the sight of him only made a difficult morning worse.

She unlocked the door and stepped aside. "Hey. I'll go get Ember for you."

"I'm not here to see Ember. I'm on my way to the food bank, but I saw your Jeep and hoped I might catch you before you got away for the day."

"OK."

"I wanted you to know that I still want the Nativity set. I didn't want our disagreement the other night to make you think I didn't."

Holly had a moment of joy over the restored commission, but it was tempered with an equal amount of hesitation at having to deal with the angel again.

I told you that you couldn't get rid of me that easily.

"Go away," she whispered.

"What?" Riley asked.

"Nothing. Just...thinking out loud." She forced a smile. "Thanks for taking the time to let me know. You'll have it in time for Christmas."

"Great. Just one more thing." He held out a card.

"What's that?" Holly asked even as her hand came out to take it from him.

"It's the address to where your parents are staying. I just thought you might want it." Before she could speak a word of denial, he turned away, climbed into a car idling at the curb, and backed out of the spot.

Holly stared at the card for a few seconds before she crumpled it in a tight fist.

"Such a nice boy."

She whirled to find Ruthie standing behind her.

"I didn't mean to scare you. Can I have a minute?"

Holly looked into the motherly face that had given her such comfort earlier and couldn't deny the request. "Sure."

With no further word or warning, Ruthie pulled her into a loose embrace. Holly looked over her shoulder. The store remained empty save for the two of them. Despite the fact that the sarcastic part of her brain yelled *setup*, she found herself returning the hug.

Ruthie's whispered words were soft against Holly's ear. "We said a prayer for you just now. I want you to know that you are an amazing young woman. To thrive after all you've endured—we need more examples like you in the world." She rubbed Holly's back. "I know you aren't a believer, but that Bible verse I quoted earlier suits you to a tee. God has a plan for your life, one drawn out before you were ever born. When you decide to look for it, I want you to know that I'm here for you. I'll be praying in the meantime." Without waiting for a response, she stepped back and walked away.

Holly watched her go, her eyes clouding with tears, an odd sense of peace in her heart.

CHAPTER ELEVEN

Riley smacked his fist against the steering wheel. He didn't claim to be an expert in female emotions, but Holly's eyes had been red and puffy. He'd bet money that she'd been crying just minutes before he arrived. It had taken every ounce of his self-control not to drag her into his arms and offer her whatever comfort she needed. His humorless snort of laughter filled the car. After Saturday night, that would probably get him slapped.

He mulled over everything she'd told him for about the millionth time while he drove. Holly claimed not to be blind or stupid.

Neither was he. Riley accepted that there would always be people who took advantage of the system, but to the degree she'd described? She'd been too adamant for him to think she was lying, but it was hard to put her words into any sort of relatable context.

He focused on the road, unable to resolve the feeling that, as bad as Holly had made her childhood sound, it was likely worse. Unable to work it out on his own, he turned to the One who always had an answer when he didn't.

"Father, I don't know what to do. You've given me a heart for society's neglected, but Holly's story planted a seed of doubt I can't seem to root out. I don't ever want to be guilty of doing more harm than good. You already know that I like this girl. I can tell that she's been deeply hurt. Show me how to be her friend, how to help her without compromising the job You called me to do."

He pulled into the parking lot and shook his head at the sight of a little sign taped to the building in front of the open spot closest to the door. *Administrator.* That was him, and from the crowded jumble of cars and the fact that the center didn't open for another thirty minutes, it looked as if the entire volunteer staff had turned out to welcome him on his first official morning.

Once he was inside, he found his assumption correct. He snagged a homemade cupcake from a platter on the desk outside his office, greeted people, and accepted handshakes and pats on the back. It would take him days to put names to the two dozen faces of his coworkers, but he'd get there. As opening time approached, the party atmosphere thinned along with the crowd. By nine, the only people who remained were the ones scheduled to work that day, and they seemed to have everything under control. He was about to look for something productive to do when the phone next to the cupcakes rang. He reached for it, but the only other paid member of the staff, the daily receptionist, beat him to it.

"Bread Basket. How can we help you?"

Riley watched as her smile broadened. "Good morning, Kate. He's standing right here, and I'm sure he can get you taken care of. Can I put you on hold for just a second?" She nodded at a response he couldn't hear, pushed a button, and replaced the receiver. "You have a call, Pastor Riley." She looked over his shoulder at the door. "And we're about to get busy and noisy in here." She motioned to his office. "Line one."

Riley hustled into his office and scooted behind his desk. Someone on the other end of that call needed help. Excitement twitched at his shoulder blades as he picked up the phone. "Pastor Riley."

"Good morning, Pastor. My name is Kate Black. I run a center that aids the families of deceased vets."

Riley had lived in Garfield for several years. Though he'd never met Kate, he was familiar with the center and the work she did there. He was also quite familiar with her husband, Chief of the Garfield Police Department, Nicolas Black. He looked down at his desk with a silent chuckle. Not his finest hour. But the theft he'd been framed for and the beating he'd taken because of it were well in the past. Valuable lessons learned and the beginning of a lifelong bond with Dane Cooper. *God always has a plan.*

Kate continued. "I've got a little problem already this morning, and I thought you might be able to help me."

"I'll certainly do what I can. What's going on?"

"When I opened this morning my first client was a widow with five children under the age of ten. Tragic story, but then they all are. They are in desperate need. We'll be doing what we can on our end to put some much-needed aid in motion, but one of their immediate needs is food. They live close to the Kansas state line, but the food bank I work with in that area is closed this week due to broken water pipes that flooded their facility over the weekend. You guys are my go-to center for local cases, but I was hoping that you could give this family some help without stretching your resources too thin."

"You send them this way. We'll hook them up."

"Oh, you are such a blessing."

Before Riley could respond, he heard a tap on the door frame and looked up to see Gilbert Hoffman. It had been less than forty-eight hours since Riley had taken him home with enough food to feed two people for a month. What could he need now? The man didn't look any better than he had on Saturday. Still haggard and dirty. Riley's gaze traveled from Gilbert's drawn face down to his worn shoes.

Worn shoes?

Riley frowned. He'd bought the man new shoes on Saturday. Why—?

"Pastor Riley?"

The sound of Kate Black's voice snapped Riley back to the

business at hand. He held up a finger and motioned his visitor into the seat across from his desk while tuning back into his conversation with Kate.

"I'm sorry, Mrs. Black—"

"Kate, please."

"Kate, I'm sorry. I had a bit of an interruption. What did you say?"

"I said that your help would be a tremendous blessing this morning."

Her words brought a smile to his face. "Thank you, it's my pleasure. Send your family my way once you're done, and we'll make sure they get what they need."

"Thank you, Pastor."

"Any time." Riley replaced the receiver and studied Gilbert for a few seconds before speaking. "Good morning, Gilbert. What brings you back to us so soon?"

The older man ducked his head and fiddled with the frayed hem of his jacket. "Just wanted to thank you again for what you did for me and the misses a couple days back."

A look crossed Gilbert's features, and the word *sly* came to mind. Was Riley letting Holly's bias color his perceptions? This was his job. This was a man who needed help. He'd do his best to give it.

"I was wondering," Gilbert continued, "if it wouldn't be too much trouble..." His feet shuffled on the tile floor. "Well, you see, the doctor left another prescription at the pharmacy for Cindy. It's forty dollars, and we just don't have it. I was hoping you could loan me the money. I'd pay you back at the first of next month when we get our check."

Riley sat back in his seat, dumbfounded at the bald-faced lie. He'd been to the pharmacy with Gilbert on Saturday. He'd seen the man's state issued insurance card. He knew the co-pay for prescriptions was closer to five, not forty. He bit his lip, stanching the automatic no that begged to escape. Logic, Holly's warning, and his servant's heart locked in a three-way battle.

It might be a medication that isn't covered by the insurance, his heart said.

I told you so, Holly's voice whispered in his ear.

Logic argued that there was only so much he could be expected to do.

Riley studied the older man. What should he do? He leaned forward as an idea took shape. "I'm sorry to hear that Cindy isn't better." He stood and dug his car keys out of his pocket. "Why don't I take you to the drug store? We'll pick up the medicine, and I can drive you home. It'll be much faster that way."

Riley did not imagine the sly look on Gilbert's face this time. After a short but intense staring match, Gilbert stood and held up a hand. "No, Pastor. That's too much trouble, and I've imposed on you enough. If you'll just loan me the money, I'll—"

"Nonsense," Riley said. "I insist."

Gilbert looked around the office. *Sly* had been replaced with *dread*. He pulled a phone from his pocket. "I need to check on Cindy before we go." He punched in some numbers and stole a few glances at Riley while he waited for the call to connect.

"Hon, it's me. How you feeling?" His head bobbed. "That's good, baby, that's good. You take it easy. I'll be home in a while." He disconnected without giving her time to respond and gave Riley a toothless smile. "Looks like we don't need your help after all. Cindy says she's feeling a lot better."

Caught you, didn't I? Out loud Riley said, "That's good news."

"Yes sir." Gilbert turned to leave. "Thanks for offering to help us again."

Riley followed Gilbert out of his office. "No problem at all." He watched the man leave the building while an idea nagged at him. He looked at the receptionist. "Everything under control here?"

"Yes, sir. We are a well-oiled machine."

"Good." He told her about the family coming in from the vet center. "I was going to take care of them in person but"—he looked out the door—"there's something I need to follow up on. I may be gone a couple of hours."

Her eyes cut to the door and back to Riley. "Something to do with your visitor?"

"Yep."

"Sounds like center business to me. Take your time."

Riley hustled out and looked up and down the street. Gilbert was long gone, but Riley refused to be deterred so easily. The bowling alley and the apartments that Gilbert and Cindy Hoffman called home were just a mile away.

He took his time on the short drive. Just a couple of blocks from his destination, he caught sight of Gilbert and pulled over. It was clear that the older man was headed home, and Riley didn't want to be seen. He scrolled Facebook on his phone for a few minutes before judging it safe to approach the decrepit old building. He staked out a position down the block and across the street that gave him a direct line of sight to Gilbert's front door.

Riley wasn't sure what he was looking for, but he didn't have long to wait. The front door to the apartment opened, and a stranger exited carrying a box that looked oddly familiar. The distance was an issue, but it almost looked like... Riley turned on his phone's camera, pointed it in the direction of Gilbert's apartment, and used the zoom feature to get a better look at what the new player in this game carried. He sucked in his breath as the box came into focus. It was one of the boxes Riley had packed full of groceries on Saturday. And from what he could see, it was still full of the items that Gilbert had *meekly* declared would see him and his wife through until their monthly aid came in.

The strange man's mouth moved in words Riley couldn't hear, but the action was self-explanatory. Gilbert moved into the picture and held out his hand. For a second Riley thought the men were about to shake. Instead the unknown man set the box on the sidewalk, dug out his wallet, and started counting out money. Had Gilbert just sold a box full of the groceries he'd claimed to need so much?

Riley put the phone down, slumped in the seat, and rested his head against the back of the seat. Holly's words rang in his ears. *You, my friend, were taken in by the biggest con artist your little center is ever likely to see.* He stared at the quiet apartment while something else she'd said nagged at him. *Drugs.* She'd mentioned a drug habit that spanned years.

A beat-up old pickup passed him and turned into the vacant parking spot directly in front of Gilbert's door. When the horn sounded, Riley grabbed his phone and zoomed in on the activity a second time. Gilbert left the apartment carrying another item that Riley had no problem identifying, the box that had held the new boots Riley had purchased to take the place of the worn tennis shoes.

He smacked the steering wheel as he watched Gilbert get into the truck.

"You old reprobate," Riley whispered. "I'd bet money the boots are still in there." Driven by an irresistible urge to see this little drama through to its conclusion, Riley started his car and followed the truck. He wasn't the least surprised to see it turn into the parking lot of the store he'd taken Gilbert to on Saturday.

Riley's breath left him in a whoosh as a single certainty filled him. Gilbert was returning the boots. He needed to be sure, so he entered the store and meandered to the service desk. He watched from around the corner as the boots were exchanged for the purchase price. He ducked out of sight when Gilbert turned to leave.

Disillusioned, Riley walked to his car. He didn't need to see any more. It figured that the sixty dollars in the older man's pocket would be spent on the drugs that Holly claimed her father couldn't live without. *Conned* was a polite word for what Gilbert had done to him.

Riley sat in the car for several minutes. He'd been so offended by Holly's words on Saturday night, her bias against the ministry he'd dedicated his life to. He stared off in the direction he'd seen the pickup take and admitted to himself that there was no such thing as a perfect system, and the food bank was no exception to that. He was sorry that Holly and her sister felt as though they'd been harmed by it. Despite that, Riley knew food banks and other similar services accomplished more good than bad. The words of his mentor pastor came back to him. "If you're not taken advantage of at least once in your ministry, you're not doing enough."

Still, that sixty dollars stung. He looked up. "Father, I bought the boots at Your prompting. I did it gladly, and I'd do it again, but why?" The answer to his question was immediate.

You needed to see for yourself. Gilbert is not the one I sent you here to help.

CHAPTER TWELVE

Holly rushed inside Ashton's Pet Rite at two minutes before five on Monday afternoon. She gave herself a handful of seconds, just inside the sliding glass doors, to catch her breath. Pet Rite was a mom-and-pop business. They employed the best dog groomers in town, but they closed promptly at five, and their overnight boarding fees were steeper than steep. The Greenbaums would not have been pleased if she'd been late picking up their two Labradoodles from their spa day.

Holly's breathing slowly returned to normal after her two-block mad dash from the only parking spot she could find. As she entered the store, the clerk minding the checkout grinned and looked down at her watch.

"Cutting it close today," she said.

Holly waved a breathless acknowledgment and headed back to the doggy beauty salon. It hadn't taken long for the emotional start to her morning to turn into *one of those days*. She'd arrived at the Cox house right after lunch to find fresh linens stacked on all five beds and a note from the lady of the house requesting that Holly change the beds and launder the dirty sheets. Not a problem. It would add an hour to her day, but that was an extra twenty bucks in her pocket, and she'd still have plenty of time to collect the dogs. Beds stripped and remade, Holly dove into the dusting and vacuuming while the thumping of the washer provided a counter beat to the music coming from her phone.

While she kept her hands busy, her mind replayed the conversation she'd had with her friends. Holly still couldn't believe that she'd allowed the story of her childhood to spill out so completely. The whole episode had been a deviation from Holly's normal keep-it-to-yourself, handle-it-yourself routine.

Had she shared too much? Would one of her friends look back on the tale and decide that Holly was somehow less deserving of friendship given her ragtag upbringing?

Even as she'd shaken the questions away, she'd been forced to admit that, although none of the issues were resolved, she felt better for having talked it out. The other women had been so ready to listen and so eager to help. Instead of judging her, they'd offered prayer. Not that Holly figured it would make any difference, but there was something freeing about not having the whole thing bottled up inside her heart any longer.

That small amount of satisfaction turned sour the moment she'd stepped into the laundry room to put the first load of sheets in the dryer and found water soaking the washroom floor. Had she overloaded the washer? If she had, would they want her to pay for the damage? Of all the things she didn't need this ranked right near the top.

Holly made it a point never to bother her clients at work, but this was an emergency. She leaned against the wall and stared at the mess. If this was on her, it was going to put a huge dent in her finances. She scrolled through her phone to find Ms. Cox's number and waited impatiently for the call to connect.

"Holly, what can I do for you?"

Holly closed her eyes and blew out a breath before answering. "I'm sorry to bother you, but there's a problem." She swallowed. "I must have overloaded the washer or something. There's water all over the floor. I'm so sorry." She bit her lip. What was the right thing to do? Make an offer up front to pay for the damage or wait and see what her client had to say?

The silence that greeted her seemed to stretch for hours. Enough time for Holly to imagine scenarios that ranged from a hundred-dollar washer repair to thousands of dollars for flooring damage. Surely they had insurance for this sort of thing. If all she had to pay was the deductible...

"That man." Ms. Cox's voice was weary. "I swear, sometimes men are more trouble than they're worth."

Holly straightened. "What?"

"It's not your fault, hon. I noticed the leak on Saturday morning and asked my husband to check it out. I was out of the house most of the day, and we had a houseful of company yesterday. I went all weekend without using the washer, which was why I had to ask you to do the beds today." A frustrated sounding sigh filled Holly's ear. "He never mentioned it, and I didn't double-check. I just assumed...well, we know what happens when you assume. Anyway, I'm sorry for the added mess."

The explanation left Holly's shoulders sagging in relief.

"Be a dear and clean up the water as best you can. I'll deal with the rest, and my husband, when I get home."

By the time the floor was dry, two baskets of water-logged towels stood by the washer, and Holly's wet jeans clung to her legs like a second skin. A glance at her watch sent her racing out the door. She had twenty minutes to make it to the dog groomer.

And here she was.

Once the dogs were delivered safe and sound, Holly climbed back into her vehicle and crossed one more thing off her Monday to-do list. The not too unpleasant scent of freshly groomed dogs lingered in the Jeep. For just a moment, her mind went back to Riley and his car on Saturday night. Her lips twitched. He'd tried so hard to eradicate the stench and failed so miserably. She really was sorry about how she'd treated him, but as far as she was concerned, their fractured-before-it-got-started friendship was just one more thing her parents had ruined.

Holly's stomach grumbled as she turned the key in the ignition. She looked at the clock in the dash. Almost six. It'd be seven by the time she got home. The Avon would take a couple of hours and, since Riley had gone out of his way to confirm that he still wanted it, the Nativity set needed some of her attention tonight. Not a lot of time left for meal prep. She sent Sage a text.

Have you had dinner?

The response was quick in coming.

Not yet. It's been a booger of a day. Have you?

Holly couldn't help the little heart leap. It sounded like friendly Sage and not the aggravated one she'd been imagining all day. She typed in a new message.

I'm in Ashton, home in 45. Pizza?

Pepperoni, extra cheese, garlic crust?

Is there any other kind? Holly answered.

You're the best sister ever!

Sage's response filled Holly's eyes with grateful tears. She remembered Piper's words from this morning. Maybe love did win in the end.

Less than an hour later, Holly stepped onto the porch, both hands underneath the large pizza box. There was no way they could eat the extra-large pie, but with two busy schedules, leftovers were always a good thing. The thirty-minute drive home with dinner sitting on the seat beside her had been torture. There were five traffic lights on the route she'd taken. Fate had turned them all red in her path. She'd spent every second of every stop doing her best to ignore the garlic and pepperoni scented steam wafting from the box. The temptation to liberate a piece and indulge right then and there had been almost unbearable.

She shifted the box and reached for the door. Before her hand made contact with the knob, Sage swung the door open.

"Thank God you're home. I'm starving." Sage held out her hands. "Give me the box and wash up. I made us a salad."

"Yes, Mom," Holly joked as she handed over the pizza. Leave it to Sage to toss greens at her when all she wanted was gooey, stringy cheese. She'd eat the salad because it was important to her sister, not because she particularly liked it. Maybe Sage would be too hungry to notice the small amount of lettuce on Holly's plate swimming in a bath of ranch dressing.

By the time she made it to the table, Sage had plates fixed for both of them. Holly took her seat, put her hands in her lap, and waited for Sage to sit. She watched her sister from under her lashes as Sage sat and bowed her head, her lips moving in a silent prayer. Holly refused to share the prayer, but she respected her sister enough to tolerate her new faith.

Respect?

Make that love. Holly loved her sister more than any other person on this earth. Sage had been there for her when no one else had. Everything else, even their current disagreement about their parents, was secondary.

"I'm sorry." The words seemed to leap from Holly's mouth the moment Sage lifted her head.

Sage studied her for a second before sliding her open hand across the top of the table. When Holly took it, she squeezed. "I'm sorry too. I didn't mean to make you mad the other night, and I didn't mean to give you the silent treatment over the weekend. I guess I just needed some time to process...to think about what Gilbert and Cindy's return might mean."

"Did you find an answer?"

Sage shook her head. "Nope. But I did come to some conclusions."

Holly pulled her hand free and picked up a slice of pizza. "Wanna share?" She took a healthy bite and waited for Sage to answer.

Sage picked up her fork and mixed her dressing into her salad, a thoughtful expression on her pretty face. "I know that the way I look at things since I got saved is confusing to you."

"Understatement," Holly mumbled around the bite she was chewing.

"But whatever I do where our parents are concerned shouldn't have any bearing on you." Holly would have objected if she hadn't had a mouth full of pizza. Sage must have seen the intent on her face because she held up her fork. "I'll make you a promise. If I decide to see them, I won't bring them here or even tell them where we're living. I won't involve you in any way that you don't agree to first. I know you're worried that they've only come back to try and worm their way into our lives. I'm not going to let that happen. Being saved doesn't make me stupid. I hope it makes me smarter."

Holly chewed in silence, not sure how to respond.

"I know that look," Sage said.

"What look?"

"That look that says you're unsatisfied with my answer and looking for a loophole. You're just going to have to trust me on this one."

"I just don't want either of us hurt."

"On that we agree." Sage tilted her head. "Are we good?"

Holly nodded, not happy that Sage hadn't promised to ignore the return of their parents as she intended to but relieved that things between them were back to normal for the moment. A little niggle of conscience pricked at her.

"Since we're clearing the air," Holly said, "you should probably know that I had a long talk with the ladies this morning."

Sage forked up a bite of salad. "About what?"

Suddenly, all of Holly's self-reassurance that Sage wouldn't care about the morning's conversation seemed pretty weak. She looked down at her lap where her hands were clenched in a white-knuckled grip. "Everything. Our argument...life with Gilbert and Cindy." She met Sage's gaze. "I'm sorry. I know it's your story, too, and I should have asked first, but I was upset and it just all tumbled out."

Sage laid the fork aside. "Did it make you feel better?"

It was a simple question, but Holly took the time to give her question the full consideration it deserved. "Yeah, it really did. Not so much about Gilbert and Cindy being back in town...but it felt good to get it off my chest. It felt better to know that none of them thought less of me because of the way we were raised."

"That's what's important. I would have liked to have been there, but if talking with our friends gave you some peace, then I'm good with it. It's not as if we had a blood oath to keep the story secret." Sage lifted a slice of the pizza and nodded at Holly's plate. "You need to eat."

Relieved that all was well and that she hadn't misjudged her sister, Holly turned her full attention to her salad. When the last scrap of green was gone, she added two more slices of pizza to her plate. "You won't think I'm horrible if I take this to my desk to finish, will you? I have Avon to do, and I need to get some work done in the garage before I go to bed."

"You go do what you need to do. I'll finish and clean up here."

CHAPTER THIRTEEN

After a disappointing morning and a hectic afternoon, Riley retired to his room right after dinner. Flat on his back atop the multicolored quilt that covered his bed, he lay with his hands behind his head and mulled the ins and outs of his day.

Gilbert is not the one I sent you here to help.

The sentence seemed lodged in his heart and his brain, repeating over and over like a broken record. It didn't take a degree in rocket science to figure out that God's target in all of this was Holly. And there was no doubt that Holly needed someone to help her. She had some serious scars from her childhood, but why him? And why did he feel this overwhelming attraction to a girl he'd just met? Something inside of him had clicked the moment he'd laid eyes on her. He'd never been a big believer in love at first sight. He'd always considered that a weird, silly concept, something girls used to describe a sudden crush. And then it happened to him.

"Love." He whispered the word into the empty room and gave himself time to taste and hear it. After several seconds, he groaned. It fit, God help him. But that couldn't be right. The girl wasn't a Christian. Her upbringing gave her no reason to respect his job and no understanding of his call to the ministry.

Riley closed his eyes and drew Holly's face into his consciousness. She was beautiful, no doubt about it. Surely, he wasn't gullible enough to fall so hard for a pretty face. He thought back to their bargaining war over the Nativity set and the unshakable confidence she had in her work. Was he mistaking admiration for love? His heart ached at the fact that she'd been so lost and hurt as a little girl. Was it compassion he was feeling? No. He discarded each of those options as quickly as the words gained substance.

Gilbert is not the one I sent you here to help.

The words circled around in his brain once more. Every logical part of his being encouraged him to take a step away from a situation so full of pitfalls, but God obviously had a plan that included Riley getting to know Holly better. The looming question boiled down to whether or not Riley could do what God wanted him to do and still protect his already compromised heart.

Riley sat up on the edge of the bed and lowered his head into his hands.

"I'm really going to need Your help and direction with this one, Father. You know I'll do my best to be obedient to what I hear You telling me to do. But we both know that a Christian falling for someone who isn't..." He glanced up, and his gaze landed on the Bible he kept on his nightstand. "That isn't in the approved handbook."

The second thing on his mind shifted to front and center. Gilbert. "I know You said that Gilbert isn't why I'm here, but the man still needs help. After what I saw this morning, I'm not sure what to do. We both know it's just a matter of time before he lands back in my office. If You could provide a little extra wisdom there, I'd be grateful."

Riley reached for his phone and checked the time. It was after eight, and the twins should be in bed. Maybe what he needed was some advice from Mom and Dad. He opened the door to his room just a crack and listened. The silence that greeted him confirmed his assumption. If the four-year-olds were awake, quiet didn't exist.

He made his way to the family room where Mom sat curled into the corner of the sofa with a book while Dane relaxed in his recliner with the TV on low. They both looked up when he stepped in.

Mom closed her book but kept her finger between the pages. "There you are. You disappeared so quickly after dinner, Dad and I figured that your first day at the center wore you to a nub."

"Hardly," Riley said. "Working at the food bank is a vacation compared to keeping up with Dad ten hours a day."

His dad's eyebrows lifted. "Don't get soft on me. Tomorrow is an early day for you, right?"

"Yes, sir. The food bank closes at three on Tuesdays."

"Good. I'll drop some lumber off in the morning. You can put in a couple of hours at the craft store once you finish at the center."

Riley must have sighed louder than he'd intended because his mom chuckled."

"He can be a slave driver, but I love him anyway."

"Yeah. I nicknamed him *Simon Legree* years ago," Riley reminded her.

His mom nodded at the memory. "That you did, but I don't think that's what brought you out of your room."

Riley took a deep breath, suddenly feeling guilty about interrupting his parents' quiet time. He'd started to make some vague excuse about what he needed when he saw Dad giving him *the look.* It was the same look he'd given a troubled fifteen-year-old Riley the day he'd rescued him from a stint in juvie—and many times since in the intervening nine years. It was like Dad could see into Riley's soul. If Riley went back to his room now, he could expect a visit from his dad before the night was out. Better to broach the issue now and be done with it.

"I could use some help if you guys aren't busy."

Dad lifted the remote from the arm of the chair and turned the TV off. Mom marked her place in the book and patted the cushion next to her.

"You've been broody for a couple of days," she said. "What's on your mind, sweetheart?"

Riley sat, unsurprised. Her mom radar had always been tuned-in to his frequency. As a child, he'd resented it more often than not, even as he'd marveled at it. As a young man, the wonder was still there, but he'd learned to appreciate it. He leaned forward and clasped his hands between his knees.

"I had an interesting visitor when I went into the food bank Saturday morning. When it happened, all I could think about, all I felt, was joy at the opportunity to do what I feel God called me to do." His shoulders slumped as the weight of being so easily deceived settled around them. He lowered his gaze to the floor, and when he continued his words were tired. "Today I learned some things that make me feel as if I've gotten this whole thing incredibly wrong."

Riley looked up when he heard Dane lower the footrest of his recliner.

Dane mirrored Riley's pose. "Tell us what happened. We'll put our heads together and see if we can't come up with some answers."

Riley was grateful for the gazillionth time that God had brought this man into their lives. He told them the whole of it. His interaction with Gilbert. The fact that he turned out to be Holly's father. Holly's reaction, complete with her unbelievable claims and unreasonable demands. His certainty that she was overreacting. His disillusionment at seeing the truth with his own eyes. He left out his confusion about what God had laid on his heart that afternoon. Some things a man just had to work out for himself.

When he finished, Riley ran his hands through his thick hair in frustration. "I don't know what to do going forward. I know the man is going to show up at the center again. Do I just pretend I don't know what I know, or do I turn him away? What happens if he has a legitimate need that I could have helped with and I didn't?" His voice dropped to a whisper. "Is this man a unique case or are there others out there just like him? Either way, how do I know who to help and who to turn away from?" His sigh was disconsolate. "This whole thing is just messed up."

Several seconds of silence passed before his mom took his hand and tugged. When he met her gaze, she smiled at him. "Can I tell you a story?"

"Yeah, I guess."

She patted his hand. "You'll enjoy this one. A few years ago, Charley had a friend who had a friend who knew a girl. This girl had a brand new baby and a really sad story. All we had was a name and an address, but Charley stepped in and rallied the troops. She organized a grocery shower and a baby shower for this girl none of us knew. I can't think of a single lady at Grace Community who didn't contribute something to the cause. Once everything was collected, Charley, Alex, and I loaded it all up and took it to Ashton. When we arrived at the house, it was easy to believe that everything we'd heard was true. The place was a hovel with ripped screens on the windows, threadbare rugs on a water stained plywood floor, and ancient, peeling paper on the walls. The baby was screaming, and the mom met us at the door in a dirty robe with a cigarette dangling from her mouth. When we told her who we were and why we were there, this young woman broke down and wept. We unloaded everything—it was a lot—and came home. We left there feeling ten feet tall and bulletproof. We'd showered the love of Christ on someone who really needed it."

Nice story, but he couldn't figure out how it applied to him. He was about to say so when Mom held up a finger to silence him.

"The story is not over yet. I kept that warm fuzzy feeling right up until I remembered I needed a birthday card for the next day. I went back to the store, and imagine my surprise when I saw the woman we'd helped not two hours earlier, the woman who'd cried while expressing her gratitude, returning the six boxes of diapers I'd bought. You got your sleuthing genes from your momma. I followed this woman from the return counter to the tobacco counter, where she exchanged the cash from the diapers for several cartons of cigarettes."

"Wow," Riley said. "That's ugly."

"That's one word for it." She locked her gaze with his, her eyes intense. "I've been in your shoes, baby. I know how hard it is to lose your innocence in a cause you believe so firmly in. But you need to remember two things."

He sat back, eager for her to share.

"Don't lose your commitment or your faith because someone else acts irresponsibly, and never, ever forget that God sees everything. He rewards you for *your* obedience, not what someone else does."

"Mom's right," Dad said. "There are always going to be people who take advantage, but that's on them, not you. I can't tell you how to do your job, but when this guy comes in again, maybe you should limit your help to what the food bank provides. I'd be surprised if there weren't some rules in place at the center that address cash handouts. If there aren't, maybe that's something you should institute before someone else gets taken advantage of." He held a hand out in the space between the recliner and the sofa. When Mom took it, he continued. "Mom and I will make the issue a matter of prayer. Both that God will have His way in... What did you say his name was?"

"Gilbert Hoffman," Riley answered.

"In Gilbert's life and that He'll give you some extra discernment in the day to day."

"Thanks, guys. That'll help a lot." Riley stood. "I love you both. I'm so glad that God made us a family when He did." He stooped to place a good night kiss on his mother's cheek and turned to find Dad on his feet. He pulled him into a hug and thumped Riley on the back.

"Mom and I are proud of you, son."

Riley returned to his room encouraged and ready to face whatever the next day tossed his way. But one question remained unanswered.

What about Holly?

He couldn't ignore what he felt for her, and he couldn't deny what he'd heard God say. How was he going to get close to her... without getting close to her?"

~

HOLLY STIFLED A YAWN. The Avon order was finished. If she got a move on, she'd be able to spend an hour on the Nativity set before she called it a day. She studied the boxes. Dread welled up in her chest at the thought of opening any of them. But maybe... She reached for the box labeled Mary. Hopefully, woman to woman, Mary would go easy on her after the day she'd had.

She placed the box on the workable, removed the lid, and held her breath. When she lifted the figurine free of the packing, she wasn't sure if she should be happy or disappointed when the only sound she heard was her own breathing. "And that's just stupid," she muttered to herself as she studied her paints, trying to decide what color to paint Mary's robe. She selected a bottle and held it up to the light. It looked almost black in the container, but it would be a deep maroon when applied.

"Thank you. I like that one a lot."

Holly almost dropped the bottle on the cement floor. Her moves to save it would have made a professional juggler proud. She clasped the little jar to her chest and closed her eyes. "I'm so glad you approve." The words were a cynical whisper, the sarcasm obviously lost on the statue.

Mary continued. "I never had anything so fine in real life. Such vibrant colors were hard to come by in my day, difficult to make and expensive. Joseph was a good husband and a wonderful provider, but when you're raising a houseful of children, their needs come before pretty things. Is it still that way?"

Mary's question pulled Holly right back into the conversation she'd had with her friends earlier in the day. When she answered, her words where terse. "I wouldn't know." She unscrewed the lid and dipped the brush into the bottle. She picked up the figurine, ready to apply the first strokes of color, but she paused for a few seconds to see if there would be any response to her comment.

Nothing.

Holly swiped the white porcelain with the brush. The color was perfect.

"Do you think it's pretty?" Even as she asked the question, Holly closed her eyes in annoyance at herself. *Stop asking questions you don't want answered. These things aren't real. You're just feeding your own delusions.* She painted in silence for several moments.

"It's lovely."

This time Holly didn't fumble anything, she just closed her eyes in frustration. "Could you do me a favor?"

"I can try."

"If you're going to talk to me, could you answer my questions when I ask? The way you come and go is really nerve-racking."

"Sorry." There was a tone of genuine apology in Mary's soft voice. "I could tell that my question about present-day parenting upset you. I went to ask Gabriel about it. He had to go ask the Father's permission before he could share the reason with me. I'm sorry that you had parents who failed to give you the love you needed."

Holly placed Mary on the table and bent down to look into the glassy white eyes. She'd go for brown there, she thought. She shook herself out of artistic mode and frowned. "Just how much do you people"—was *people* the correct word?—"know about me?"

Mary spread her arms and swished her half-painted robe as she answered. "Well the Father knows everything of course. Gabriel knows what he needs to know to complete the mission. The rest of us are just here to tell you the story. I wouldn't normally know more than that, but Gabriel thought, and the Father agreed, that I might be able to help you with the parent thing. Gabriel told me the whole story."

"Marvelous." Sarcasm, again, her favorite defense mechanism. Again Mary seemed not to notice it.

"I wanted to tell you that, even in my day, parenting was hard, especially if you were unprepared. Joseph and I expected to have a family, but we didn't expect to have a baby so soon. We barely had time to get to know each other before we had this little person to take care of. It was a difficult adjustment. We made our share of mistakes."

"Wasn't your *little person* a God in human form? How bad could you mess that up? Couldn't Jesus just...I don't know...snap His fingers and fix whatever mistakes you made?" Holly added a few swipes of color while she waited for an answer.

Mary laughed, the sound full of sincere delight. "People have the strangest ideas. Jesus came to earth to go through the process of being human, cradle to grave. To know what we go through every step of our lives, the good, the bad, and the ugly. He wanted to be able to have compassion on us in every situation. Experience in the temptations we all face. Answers for all the questions that plague us." Mary pointed to her skirt. "I think you missed a spot."

As Holly dabbed on more paint, Mary continued. "I've heard stories about how He healed His playmates as a toddler, how He brought dead pets back to life, how His father and I had to keep Him in the house so He wouldn't"—she waved her fingers—"use His powers when He shouldn't."

Holly rotated Mary to get to the back of her robe. "None of those things are true?"

"Of course not. I promise you that He was a normal baby through and through. A dirty-diapers, spit-up-milk, keep-me-awake-all-night baby. And later He was a skinned-knee, frog-catching, dirt-eating, tree-climbing, wrestle-with-His-brothers little boy. He had to experience the wonder, joy, angst, and pain of all those things to accomplish what He came to us to do."

"And that was...?"

The statue's head turned to look at Holly over her shoulder. "Holly, He died to make a way for us to be with Him and the Father for eternity, but He lived the life of a human so that He could comfort us through all the things we face. From birth to death, He experienced it all so we would know we were never alone."

She turned back around, and Holly had to strain to hear the whispered words that followed. "Now that I know your story, I think He might have experienced one mishap just so He could help people like you."

Mary's words halted Holly's brushstrokes mid-swipe. "What do you mean?"

"Turn me around so I can see you better. I'm getting a crick in my neck."

Holly obliged, again stooping down to be eye-to-eye with Mary. "I'm listening."

"Even after all these years, it's hard to talk about. I'm going to try because I think it will help you understand how flawed we humans can be as parents." The little statue's shoulders rose and fell in a deep sigh. "According to custom, we had to travel to Jerusalem every year to celebrate the Passover. It was a long journey and a huge undertaking, especially for families like ours with young children. We generally traveled with a large group of extended family and friends. The children loved it because it meant a break from chores and studying. It gave them a chance to see playmates they only saw once a year.

"The year Jesus was twelve, we made the traditional pilgrimage. Everything was fine until the day we started home. We didn't see Jesus all that day, but we didn't worry. He was an active, social young man, we assumed He was busy with playmates. It wasn't until we were making camp for the night and Jesus didn't come to dinner that we knew something was wrong. We began to search." Mary's voice broke, and she had to pause for a moment. "We looked everywhere but couldn't find Him. Joseph and I finally had to accept that we'd left our son in Jerusalem." The little statue bowed her head over her wringing hands. "Joseph and I were both panicked. We had to leave the other children with our family and hustle back to the city. It took us three days of searching to find Him, the longest three days of my life. You just don't know what your imagination can conjure up until you've lived through something like that. We'd just about given up hope when we looked inside the temple, and there He was." Mary put her hand over her heart. "I can't tell you how relieved His father and I were. I hugged Him so tightly. I didn't let Him out of my sight again until we got back to Nazareth."

"Careful," Holly scolded, using the tip of the brush to move Mary's arm down and away. You're still wet." She touched up the small blotch. "And you think this story applies to me?"

"I do. I know you've gone your whole life feeling scared and neglected by your parents. Jesus knows what those feelings feel like."

"But you came back for Him. You didn't make a habit of neglecting Him."

"You're right, but the point is that because He went through that experience, He knows what you're going through. He can help you put all the hurts of your childhood behind you. All you have to do is open your heart and accept what He is so willing to give." Mary sighed. "I was supposed to tell you about being a frightened, pregnant teenager in a society where that could earn you a death penalty. About having faith to believe the unbelievable, but I wanted to have this conversation with you instead. Did it help?"

Holly's response was a noncommittal "Hmmm..." as she lifted the figurine off the table. Mary's pain had come through her story loud and clear. And Holly certainly sympathized with a lost little boy, but it was impossible to compare Mary's story to hers in a meaningful way. Mary and Joseph had made an effort. Gilbert and Cindy never had. All the stories in the world couldn't fix what they'd broken. "Thanks for sharing, but I don't see what difference it makes now. I'm a grown woman. Nothing you say or do is going to change the past."

The little statue shook her head. "It's not about changing the past. It's about changing the future. That's all I want you to take away from our time together. Forgiveness is never an easy journey, but my Son can help you get there if you'll let Him."

Where was the point of arguing further? Holly opened the kiln and turned away from the quick burst of heat that washed over her face. She slid Mary inside and sealed the door. Once again, Holly's emotions were trapped in a tug-of-war between a pretty story she almost wanted to believe and the ugly reality she'd lived.

CHAPTER FOURTEEN

Tuesday was one of those rare September Oklahoma days. The heat never took a firm hold, leaving the temperature hovering around seventy-five degrees instead of the ninety of the day before, and if you breathed just right, you could smell a hint of fall in the air. It was too lovely to be inside for the whole day, so when lunchtime rolled around, Riley took himself to the nearest drive-through and picked up a burger, a large order of fries, and a strawberry shake. Food in hand, he made his way to Ashton's municipal park. He wasn't the only one with that idea.

Surrounded by stores, offices, and apartment buildings, the park was full of people taking advantage of the weather. The playground teemed with mothers and preschoolers. The noise of childish laughter mixed with parental cautions as Riley made his way through the chaos. There were a dozen or so cement picnic tables sprinkled around the park's perimeter, all of them occupied.

Feeling a bit like the new kid in a strange school, Riley perused the crowd looking for someone he recognized. He was determined to enjoy an hour in the sun. A solitary patch of grass under a tree would work, but a bit of friendly conversation wouldn't hurt his feelings either. His gaze raked the tables and snapped back to the one next to the empty basketball court.

A single occupant, lunch on a napkin, head bent over her phone. A sudden puff of breeze whipped through, rustling the leaves of the trees and throwing the woman's curly auburn hair into her face. Riley smiled when she laid her phone next to her sandwich, gathered the errant tresses in both hands at the nape of her neck, and slid a band from her wrist to restrain them. Oblivious to the observation, Holly went back to her food and her phone.

Riley watched her from the shadows for a few seconds while his heart did a jittery dance. What was it about this woman that had his mouth going Sahara dry while his pulse rate doubled? He wanted the chance to get to know her better, and he needed that to happen if he was going to find a way to help her as he felt God directing. But she'd been so... He searched for a word to attach to her behavior Saturday night. So many emotions had come pouring out of her. Anger, hurt, fear, shock. He wasn't sure which one took precedence, but he was sure he wasn't at the top of her list of favorite people.

Some motion or sound drew Holly's attention away from her phone. Her head came up, and her eyes locked with his. Caught like a stalker in the act, Riley's face heated.

"Hey," he said. "What are you doing in Ashton on this perfect day?

"My afternoon housecleaning gig is a couple of blocks away from here. You?"

Riley lifted his lunch. "Just looking for a place to sit with my food. I guess I picked a bad day for a picnic."

Holly scanned the area. When she faced Riley again, she did so with an uncertain smile. "It's the perfect day for a picnic, which is why it's so crowded. You can share my table if you want."

The offer surprised Riley, and it took a few seconds to convince his feet that he'd heard her correctly.

"Thanks." He crossed the distance and slid onto the bench across from her. More nervous in her presence than he cared to admit, he took his time with his food, unwrapping the burger, smoothing the paper out, and dumping the fries on one corner. He said a quick, silent prayer over his meal, added a request for God to bless this unexpected opportunity, took a bite of the burger, and chased it with the shake. His taste buds sent happy feelings up to his brain while his stomach urged him to hurry up and swallow already.

He looked up when Holly laughed. "What?"

"The look on your face," she said. "You look like you've been stranded on a desert island without food or drink for a week."

"I'm a growing boy." He swirled fries in ketchup. "Besides, burger and fries, the great American lunch." He stared across the table at what looked suspiciously like a peanut butter and jelly sandwich. "And food for an actual grownup." He held the burger across the table. "You want a bite?"

Holly looked from him to the burger and back. "No thanks. I wouldn't want to stunt your growth."

"Suit yourself."

They both ate in silence for a few seconds and then spoke over each other.

"I'm sorry about—" Holly began.

"I want to apologize—" Riley said.

They gazed into each other's eyes and then looked away. Silence returned to the table while they chewed.

Finally, Riley cleared his throat and made a motion with his hand. "Ladies first."

Holly finished off the crunchy Cheetos lying on the napkin next to her sandwich. With a fingertip, she shoved the leftover orange crumbs into a neat little pile. She used her last bite of peanut butter and jelly sandwich to blot them up before popping the whole thing into her mouth. Riley's expression must have given away his distaste.

"Don't knock it till you try it." She wadded up the paper and tucked it into the brown bag at her side. "I'm sorry about how upset I got on Saturday night. When you mentioned my parents, it brought up some very painful memories. I reacted badly. You have a job to do, and I'm sure you do it well. I don't have to like it or even approve of it, but I should respect it and you. You're not to blame for the actions of my parents, and I'm sorry I took it out on you. Despite what I said the other night, I know food banks and similar services are a valuable and necessary part of our society." The expression on her face tightened with what Riley identified as strain. When she continued, her words were a whisper. "I'm learning that there are no perfect parents in the world."

Talk to her now.

Riley sent a glance up to a pristine blue sky before allowing his gaze to rest on Holly once again. "I'm sorry too. I knew you were upset. It's only natural to vent. I should have let you do that instead of making things worse by trying to justify the work I do." He stretched his hand across the table and waited until Holly took it. "Friends?"

She slid her palm against his and gripped. "I'd like that."

Riley looked at their clasped hands and realized anew that he wanted so much more than friendship with this woman, wanted it so badly it was a physical pain in his chest. But there was much to do first. He gave her hand a squeeze, not letting it go.

"I know something about bad parents," he said. "My father—not Dane—was a harsh, bigoted man who ruled our home with an authority many would call abusive. I know he loved me in his own way, but he was a product of his upbringing. When Dane came into our lives, I had a lot of baggage to sort through before I could accept the love he offered. You want to know the first thing I had to do?"

When Holly gave a slight nod of her head, he continued. "I had to forgive my dad before I could move forward to the good things God had planned for me." He tightened his grip on her hand when she tried to pull away and waited until she stilled to continue. "It wasn't easy, but as bad as I had it"—his mind went back to the blatant dishonesty he'd witnessed the day before—"I'm thinking you had it worse. You probably have a lot more to forgive than I can even imagine."

~

The kindness and understanding in Riley's words clawed deep gashes in Holly's already tender heart. Yesterday's conversation with her friends. The continued uncertainty about what Sage intended to do. Last night's lecture from Mary. Now Riley. It was too much. Holly disengaged her hand, clasped it in her other, and bowed her head over them. Why couldn't everyone just leave her alone and let things go back to normal? A tear plopped on her clenched fingers and she rushed to wipe it away.

"Holly, please look at me."

She sniffed and fished the used napkin out of the bag. She didn't look up until she'd blotted her face and was sure she had control of her emotions.

Riley's face bore a sympathy that threatened to undo that control. "I know how impossible forgiveness can seem, especially when the person we need to forgive seems unworthy of it. But you have to remember that you aren't forgiving them for their sake, you're forgiving them so you can live your best life. Holding all that hurt inside will eventually leach every drop of happiness out of your life."

"I don't want to see them, much less speak to them." Holly's voice was a ragged whisper. "Why is that so hard for everyone to understand?"

Riley tilted his head and studied her. "Is that what's holding you back?"

Holly bobbed her chin.

"You don't need to speak to them to forgive them. You don't have to be in the same room with them. You don't have to be on the same planet with them. My father was dead when I finally asked God to help me forgive him. And that's the key, Holly. God is the only One who can help us do the things we can't do on our own. If we come to Him and accept the gift of His Son, He'll forgive us and help us get beyond the pain of our past. But you have to ask for His help because He's a gentleman. He isn't going to barge into your life and take over. Trust me, sometimes I wish it were that easy."

Holly shifted her gaze from his face to stare over his right shoulder. "I don't believe the same way you do. Even if I did, I'm tired of being preached at."

Riley's confusion was obvious. "Who's preaching at you?"

"Gab—," Holly covered her mouth and coughed to cover the near slip. She wasn't going there with Riley or anyone else. "Lots of people," she mumbled from behind her hand. "It's monotonous."

"I can see where it would be." He swung his legs over the cement bench and stood. "I've got to get back to the center. Do two things for me, would you?"

"What?"

"Think about what I said, really think. If you have questions, you know where to find me. I'll help as best as I can."

I don't need help, I need peace. The thought trembled on her lips, begging for release. But they'd just made up one argument. She didn't want to start another. "OK," she said aloud. "And?"

"Have dinner with me Saturday night. I think we deserve a do-over. I promise I won't talk about any of this unless you bring it up."

"How about a *yes* to the second and an *I'll try* on the first?"

Riley circled the table and stood behind her. He put his hands on her shoulders. "That works." He bent down to place a quick kiss on the top of her head. The contact lingered as the kiss turned into an awkward hug. "You're a special person, Holly Hoffman, very special, to me and to God. I'll call you later in the week to set up plans for Saturday."

He was gone before Holly had the chance to respond. She shifted in her seat and watched him hustle back to his car. Her hand trembled as she touched her hair where his lips had rested a few short seconds ago. Holly appreciated the sweetness of the gesture. Non-threatening. Nothing required in return. Just a moment of connection.

She licked her lips and wondered what his mouth on hers

would feel like, taste like. Heat bloomed in her belly and spread through her extremities like a brushfire in August. The intensity of her reaction took her by surprise. Her feelings for Riley were more than a little conflicted. She liked him, no doubt there. He was handsome and thoughtful and funny. He was also a Christian, one called into a ministry of helping others.

She was neither.

The realities of those last two things should have kept them out of each other's orbit. Instead, they seemed to be spinning closer each time they met.

Holly didn't understand.

Maybe he considered her a project, like one of the people he worked with at the food bank. Maybe he thought she needed a kind word or a Christian Band-Aid to stop the bleeding of a wounded heart.

Was it pity? Was that what had him asking her out again?

She'd had enough of that to last a lifetime. Didn't need or want any more, yet the memory of Riley's parting words and the hug that came with them...those hadn't felt like pity.

You're a special person, Holly Hoffman, very special, to me and to God.

Holly doubted Riley passed out hugs and kisses to his clients at the food bank. That image had her laughing out loud as she swung her legs over the bench and stood. She had one more house to clean and a list of dogs to walk this afternoon before calling it a day. There would be plenty of time to think about some of the things he'd said before going home to work on the Nativity set.

One house, six dogs, and five hours later, Holly made her way out to the garage. Sage would be late, and her message said she'd bring dinner. That gave Holly a couple of uninterrupted hours to paint. She studied the boxes and selected the one labeled *wise man*.

She could use a little wisdom. Maybe he'd dole some out.

Holly braced herself as she took the figurine out of the box and sat it on the table. She studied it, making mental notes for paint selection. Where Gabriel's robe was lovely and flowing, it was simple in design. Mary's tunic also had very little ornamentation. This little guy had an elaborate turban, chains around his neck, and several layers of clothing. He was so different from the other characters that Holly had taken the time to google the wise men from the Christmas story. Now she knew that he was dressed as the foreign man of position and wealth he was purported to be. She turned to her rack of paints and picked out the colors she wanted. Lots of gold here for the jewelry and the gift he carried. Purple, green, and brown for the cape and robe. When she turned back to the table she was surprised, but not as shocked as she would have been a week before, to find the little man bowing in her direction.

"Good day, Mistress Holly. Allow me to introduce myself. I am Melchior of Persia, one of the three Magi who made the journey to honor the Christ child with gifts and worship." He straightened. "My two companions, Gaspar and Balthazar, would have been thrilled to make your acquaintance, but alas, they were damaged in a shipping accident and discarded. Like the others who have come before me, I am here to tell you my story."

Holly set the selection of paints to the side and gave a small bow of her own. "Nice to meet you. Sorry to hear about your friends." She settled herself on a stool. "The work on you is going to be pretty intricate. I think we should have our talk before I get started. That way, I won't mess you up." She waved a hand in his direction. "Make it quick. I only have about two hours."

"As you wish." Melchior's expression took on a thoughtful air. "I was raised and educated in Persia, where part of our history is closely tied to the people of Israel. The Israeli people were captives of the Babylonian Empire when Babylon fell to the Persians. Since several of the captives became noblemen and rulers in our nation, their history, along with some of their traditions, became a part of our education."

Holly put her feet up on the rung of the stool. She had a feeling Melchior had a lot to learn about the words *make it quick*.

"Because of this, my friends and I knew the prophecy

concerning the Jewish Messiah and how he was destined to come to earth. When we saw that unusual star in the sky, we knew the time had come for prophecy to be fulfilled, and we began the arduous journey to Jerusalem."

Melchior tilted his head. "I've always found what happened next gravely puzzling." With his hands clasped behind his back, he paced along the edge of the table like a teacher lecturing a class. "When we arrived in Jerusalem and inquired about the child, no one knew what we were talking about. We were granted an audience with King Herod. We could tell the news of a new king troubled him when he called in the religious leaders and demanded answers. It was from them that we learned that the Christ child would be found in Bethlehem. We continued our trip with the star as our guide and finally came to the house where the child was."

"Child? He wasn't a baby?"

"No, mistress. We followed the star for many months before we arrived in Bethlehem. Jesus was a toddler when we finally found him."

Holly leaned forward, surprised to find that she was actually enjoying Melchior's story. "What part did you find puzzling?"

"Why, the part that had us traveling for months to investigate a vague part of our ancient history only to find the people who should have known the prophecy all their lives seemingly ignorant of the details. It definitely took us back, but the end of the journey made it all worth it."

"What happened then?"

"We saw the promised Messiah with our own eyes. We heard the story of how the ancient words were fulfilled from the people who lived it. It was awe-inspiring. I don't know if you appreciate just how blessed you are to experience it much the same way."

Holly stared down at the little man. *Blessed* was not the word she'd use to describe these surreal encounters.

"I see doubt on your face, mistress. There was doubt on many of the faces in Herod's throne room the day we visited. I have only three words for you, but they are very important words."

She braced herself for some deep insight. "Okay."

"It's all real."

With that, Melchior fell silent and still. He'd said his piece, and nothing Holly did as she painted him aroused him again. Later that night, while Holly lay in bed, she couldn't stop going over the story and the wise man's final words. *It's all real.* She wrestled with those words and finally ended up whispering the first prayer of her life.

"Jesus, I can't seem to get away from You lately. Don't take this conversation as an indication that I'm ready to surrender to the faith that Riley preaches and Sage embraces. But if You're up there and as real as Melchior said You are, can You help me work some of this out in my mind?"

The words echoed in the room as Holly closed her eyes to the image of a satisfied Gabriel smiling and nodding in approval.

CHAPTER FIFTEEN

"Get back here you stupid dog." The mumbled words snapped Holly out of dreamland on Saturday morning. Disoriented, she lay there for a few seconds, caught somewhere between wakefulness and sleep. Once it registered that she was safe in her own bed and not giving chase to an out-of-control hound she sighed sleepily and turned to cuddle her pillow. The groan that issued from her throat brought her to full and uncomfortable consciousness.

Yesterday had been a train wreck of a day, and this morning every muscle in her body hurt. What should have been a pleasant walk in the park with a new dog client, an adorable collie-German shepherd mix, had turned ugly when the big dog had taken off after a pair of squirrels. Lulled into a false sense of security by the dog's previously gentle demeanor, she'd been unprepared when he bolted.

The initial lunge nearly yanked her arm out of the socket, and she'd been unable to disentangle herself from the leash before she was dragged to her knees. Once she'd regained her footing, she'd been forced to run after the fool dog, limping and yelling his name like a crazy person. When the tongue lolling, tail wagging, miscreant finally came bounding back to her as if nothing had happened, she'd been tempted to strangle him.

It was all in a day's work, and there'd been no lasting damage if you didn't count her pride and a pair of ruined jeans. But this morning she felt like she'd been put through an old-fashioned wringer washer...twice.

There were days when a nice nine-to-five office job looked mighty appealing.

Holly shut that thought down before it had a chance to sprout. She enjoyed what she did and the flexibility that came from being her own boss.

And because she was her own boss, Holly decided to award herself with a hard-earned mental health day. No laundry, no cleaning, no chatty Nativity set. Instead of chores she'd spend some quality time with her Kindle. Her favorite author's newest book in the series she was reading should have been delivered overnight. She couldn't wait to dive in, and even though she'd been waiting for this new book for months, there would be very little savoring as she plowed through the story with the same restraint as a starving man confronted with a box of chocolates.

Riley was picking her up at seven, and she'd already decided on her outfit for their date. A pair of black leggings with a silky, long-sleeved tunic in a silver-gray fabric that shimmered when she moved. New shoes would be a nice addition. Holly considered her options. Sage had great taste in shoes but absolutely hated the mall. But if Holly offered to buy lunch at her sister's favorite deli, Sage might agree to help her.

Reading, lunch, shopping, reading, dinner, more reading.

Sounded like a plan.

Her caffeine alarm jangled, and her stomach growled, prompting her to look at the clock. Almost eight-thirty. Holly tossed the sheet aside, eased her aching body out of bed, and pulled on jeans and a T-shirt. She'd start the day with a little breakfast bribery.

If Holly cooked, Sage would insist on cleaning up, leaving

Holly no choice but to take a second cup of coffee and snuggle in with that new book. Plus broaching the subject of shoe shopping while Sage had a plate of hot, crispy waffles in front of her was a sound strategic move.

Holly limped down the hall and into the kitchen where she turned on the coffee, started bacon frying in a skillet, and mixed up some waffle batter. When Sage sauntered into the kitchen fifteen minutes later, breakfast was halfway done.

Sage fixed her own mug and leaned against the counter. "Smells great in here. What can I do to help?"

"Not a thing." Holly poured batter into the hot waffle iron and closed the lid. "Have a seat. This will be ready in a second."

Sage yawned and mumbled her thanks. "This is a nice treat. I'll take the clean-up after we eat."

"That works." Holly turned back to the waffle iron with a satisfied smile. It was a great feeling when a plan came together.

Five minutes later, Sage looked up from a plate of crispy bacon and a syrup-drenched waffle. "You make the best waffles I ever ate." She cut a second bite and swirled it in syrup before popping it in her mouth. She continued as she chewed, her hand covering her mouth. "So tonight's your big dinner with Riley."

"Yep."

"Excited?"

"Mostly. I figure the odds are on my side. It has to turn out better than last week," Holly said.

"I hope so. Have you got plans for rest of your day?"

"Oh, I have a few ideas," Holly answered.

"Care to share?"

Holly broke her bacon into tiny pieces and sprinkled them over her waffle.

Sage lifted an eyebrow. "What are you, five?" she teased.

Holly ignored her. The taste of waffles, maple syrup, and bacon in every bite was an unbeatable combination in her book. She'd gotten over Sage's reaction years ago. "You go first, then I'll tell you how your plans fit into mine."

Sage didn't answer right away. She kept her head bowed over her breakfast. Holly's only clue that Sage had heard her question were the deep wrinkles between her eyebrows. Whatever answer her sister was chewing on appeared to be tougher than the waffles.

Sage finally looked up, her bottom lip caught between her teeth. There was uncertainty in her voice when she spoke. "I was planning to bake a cake this morning, and I wanted to go into Ashton this afternoon."

Hmm. Sage's plans dovetailed nicely with the loose schedule Holly had set for herself, not to mention the added bonus of cake, but something in Sage's demeanor had Holly's defenses jumping to red alert. "And…?" she prompted.

Sage took a deep breath. "I've been praying about it for a week. I know you're against it, but I feel like I need to try and initiate some contact with Gilbert and Cindy."

Holly sat back, her breakfast feast forgotten while the few bites she'd already eaten threatened to make a reappearance.

Sage hurried into the silence. "I know I promised not to include you in my plans. But…" Sage's voice broke, and she pulled in a shuddering breath. When she continued, there was an uncommon hint of fear in her voice. "The thing is, I don't know that I can do this without you."

"There's no way—"

"Hear me out, please. I'm not asking you to speak to them. I'm not sure I'll speak to them today. I just want to drive by their apartment, leave a cake on their doorstep and maybe a note with my cell phone number." She blew a breath out through pursed lips. "If I do it that way, the ball will be in their court. I need you to go with me for moral support."

"How much moral support do you think I can provide when I disagree—vehemently disagree—with your plan?"

"More than you think."

Sage looked away and swallowed while Holly did her best to ignore the threat of tears in her sister's voice.

"I've really been praying about this." Sage turned back to

Holly. "I know you don't understand where I'm coming from. But I think that God wants me to make this effort, for me more than for them."

Holly closed her eyes when Sage's words echoed both Mary's and Riley's. She didn't know whether to feel resentful and ganged up on or to give up and embrace the majority opinion. When she met Sage's gaze once more, her sister's eyes were filled with anxiety and pleading. Sage had always been her rock, the one person Holly could count on when everyone else walked away. As distasteful as this request might be, how could Holly refuse to give Sage the support she'd always gladly given Holly?

"But..." Sage's smile was unsteady, and her attempt to lighten her voice failed. "I'll understand if you can't do it. Maybe this is God's way of teaching me to rely on Him in tough situations."

Holly stared at Sage for several seconds. "I don't have to get out of the car?"

Sage shook her head, and the imploring look on her sister's face left Holly feeling trapped in a situation she wanted no part of. "When do you want to leave?"

The relief that transformed Sage's expression almost made Holly's capitulation worth it. Almost.

"Not till late morning. I have to bake the cake first."

"You're gonna owe me big."

"Name it."

"I was going to buy you lunch today and ask you to go shoe shopping." She leaned forward and tried to put her most stern expression on her face. "Lunch is now on you."

"Deal."

"Plus"—Holly lifted a finger and upped the ante—"a trip to the mall with two hours of complaint-free shoe shopping."

Sage pinched the bridge of her nose and squinted as if in physical pain. "One hour."

Holly didn't feel the least bit guilty about pressing her advantage. "Remember I said *big*. Two hours, take it or leave it."

"You're a brat."

Holly ignored the jibe, pushed her barely eaten breakfast away, and stood. "Awesome. Kitchen is yours. I have a book to read."

~

HOLLY PARKED her Jeep across the street from the dilapidated group of apartments at eleven forty-five Saturday morning. She scrunched down in her seat and looked at Sage. "This is your show."

"Right." Sage climbed from the car, opened the back door, and extracted the cake she'd baked in a disposable pan. With a quick look in both directions, she crossed the street and made her way to the apartment number Riley had given to Holly earlier in the week.

Holly watched as Sage placed the cake in front of the door, knocked, and hustled back across the street. Sage reclaimed her seat, slammed the door, and clasped Holly's hand in hers.

Holly glanced down at the gesture and the surprising clamminess of Sage's hand. Sage's hand tightened around Holly's, and her breath caught. Sage's face was as white as the frosting on the cake she'd just delivered.

"What is it?"

Sage, her eyes wide with a fear Holly didn't understand, nodded across the street. Holly turned to watch the apartment door open. A skinny man dressed in shabby, oversized clothes bent down to pick up the cake. He looked around in obvious confusion. She would not have recognized him as her father if she hadn't been looking for him.

Holly was surprised at the lack of feeling seeing him again generated. Maybe eight years of independence had lessened her trepidation. Maybe she'd just grown up enough to realize that he had no further control over her. Either way, seeing him in such an obvious state of dereliction had no effect on her at all.

Nevertheless she slid further into the seat, just barely able to see over the door as he continued to scope out the area. When nothing caught his attention, he lifted the corner of the flimsy plastic cover, and swiped a finger through the frosting. The breeze snatched the cover and the small piece of paper containing Sage's contact info, which she'd taped to the inside, and sent them tumbling across the scruffy grass that fronted the row of apartments.

Holly heard the crackle of the plastic as it bounced across the street and came to rest just under her left front tire.

Gilbert took a single step forward while Holly held her breath. Another puff of wind blew the lid into the overgrown yard on the other side of the Jeep. Gilbert waved his hand in a whatever gesture, opened the door, and disappeared inside.

"We have to go." Sage's words were a strangled whisper.

"He didn't get your number."

"I don't care. I can't do this. I may never be able to do this." Sage let her head fall over her knees as she whispered what must have been a prayer. "I'm sorry, Father. I tried." She looked at Holly, her eyes wide, frightened, and full of tears. "Take me home."

"But—"

"I know you had other plans. I know I promised to go with you, but I can't." Sage reached for the door handle. "If you really need shoes that badly you'll have to go without me. I'll go over to the bowling alley and call someone to take me home."

"Stay in the car. Of course I'll take you home." Holly started the Jeep and edged away from the curb. Sage's reaction made no sense. Holly'd been the one to be afraid, but *afraid* didn't begin to cover the look on Sage's face. "But you have to trade one promise for another."

Sage cocked an eyebrow.

"You have to promise me that you're going to explain what this was about."

Sage bent her head and clasped her arms around her stomach. She stared out the window for several seconds. "I can't do that."

Holly kept her eyes on the road, but her teeth ground together in frustration at Sage's refusal to explain.

Sage said, "It's ancient history. There's no purpose in dredging it up. The good news is that I won't be seeking out Gilbert and Cindy. Today gave me the answer I've been looking for. God wanted me to offer forgiveness. I thought I was ready to do that, but now I know that's an olive branch I can't extend."

She shifted in the seat, and Holly risked a glance in her direction, appalled by the despair on her sister's face.

"It's sad really," Sage whispered. "God forgave me for so much." Her voice broke. "And I can't find it in my heart to do the one thing He's asked me to do for Him."

Holly drove while her mind raced. Why was Sage beating herself up? As far as Holly was concerned this had been a doomed mission from the start. And God? God was no help. Suddenly Riley's words came back to her. *You don't need to speak to them to forgive them.* She swallowed, feeling more than a little out of her depth. She wasn't sure she believed those words, but if they could help Sage...

"You know, I have it on good authority that forgiveness doesn't have to happen face to face."

Sage sniffed. "What do you mean?"

"Riley told me an interesting story the other day." Holly relayed his words about how he'd forgiven his father. "After hearing what he had to say, it seems to me that forgiveness might be less about one-on-one interaction with the offender and more about the intent of the forgiver. I'm not an expert in anything Christian," Holly said, feeling her way through her explanation as she went. "But if Riley is right, forgiving his father was more for his sake than his father's. More about letting go of years of hurt than making the person who hurt him feel better. If that's true, then the same applies here. Maybe God..." She took a deep breath, incredulous at the words coming out of her mouth. But she'd do just about anything to erase the pain etched on Sage's face. "Maybe you misunderstood. Not about the forgiving but about the seeing."

The rest of the ride home was silent. Sage continued to stare out the window, leaving Holly to replay her thoughts and words in her head. She wasn't just remembering Riley's words. There was the prayer she'd prayed a few nights before. Maybe everything she'd said to Sage applied to her as well.

Holly pulled into their drive, and Sage was out of the Jeep in a flash. She circled the vehicle, pulled Holly in for a tight hug, and then rushed up the porch steps.

"What's your hurry?" Holly called out from several paces behind her. She hoped that the silence on the drive home didn't mean that Sage was still upset.

"I need to call my pastor's wife. I want to tell her what you said and see what she has to say about it. Then I want to look up some scriptures on forgiveness." Sage paused in the doorway and turned. "Right now, I think you're just about the smartest little sister in the whole world."

As Sage disappeared into the house, Holly considered that. Smart? How smart was it to spout off a bunch of stuff she didn't really believe?

CHAPTER SIXTEEN

With shoe shopping canceled, Sage locked in her room, and hours before her dinner with Riley, Holly settled onto the sofa intent on salvaging the rest of her day with a healthy dose of her favorite author. She pulled her bare feet up onto the cushions, shifted until she found her reading sweet spot, and opened her Kindle. After just two short pages, her empty stomach reminded her of the lunch she'd missed. She hopped up and went into the kitchen to prowl for a snack. Five minutes later, she returned to the sofa with a soda and a bag of cheese puffs.

She climbed back into the story, determined to forget anything except the two characters running for their lives after witnessing a murder. Heart pounding, Holly swiped the screen for the next page. But her attention was ripped from the story by the orange fingerprints left on the screen.

"Good grief." Holly closed the bag, licked her fingers clean and used the hem of her shirt to clean off the reader. Eating could wait, the suspense could not. She rearranged the throw pillows, stretched out full length, and started again. Half a page later, a text chimed on her phone. The Kindle landed on her chest as her arms went lax at her sides. Was some uninterrupted reading time really so much to ask?

Holly raised her hips off the sofa and pulled the phone from the back pocket of her jeans.

DMV Announcment: Congrats on keeping your automotive record clean. Click hear to claim your $500.00 reward.

She frowned at the misspelled words and the link provided. Spam. "Do people really fall for this stuff?" Her fingers typed in a quick response.

Learn to write and speak English.

Holly hit send, dropped the phone, and collapsed back into the cushions. Maybe taking a day off when she had work she could be doing was just a pipe dream. She turned her head and stared in the direction of the garage, where the Nativity set awaited her attention.

She could almost hear the characters calling to her through the walls. She was a little surprised that the chatty angel had been so quiet over the last few days. Holly pinched the bridge of her nose.

Maybe she was going Looney Tunes, but the fact that the figurines were talking to her didn't bother her anymore. Not much, anyway.

That realization sent a snort of disbelieving laughter ricocheting around the room.

Maybe she was crazier than she'd thought, but it wasn't so much that they talked that had her hesitating to get the job done. It was their continued effort to convince her that a God who'd never shown a second's interest in her or her problems suddenly had all the answers. It was beyond ludicrous.

She sat up. Maybe she could just work on the donkey. How bad could it be? Her recent conversation with the cow shoved into her memory and answered that question. The only sure thing would be that he would have plenty to say.

Holly gave up the battle and went out to the garage. Melchior and Mary sat on the worktable. Neither figurine was completely finished, but the project was taking shape. Seeing them made Holly curious to see the rest of the set to assess her progress. She pulled the boxes from the shelf and arranged the statues in a half circle.

The second she stood the angel on the table, his wings rippled, and his hands landed on his hips. "I was beginning to think I'd never see the outside world again."

"I'm not in the mood today. If you want to keep breathing the air of the unconfined, keep quiet."

The angel crossed his arms and gave her an indignant look, but he took the hint and closed his mouth.

She reached for a jar of brown paint and a brush and picked up the donkey. The sensation as she fell into his thoughts was like the first drop on a roller coaster. Breathtaking and out of control. When she opened her eyes, instead of being surrounded by the walls of the garage, she found herself on a dirt pathway with several other travelers. The dust being kicked up by their passage was thick and gritty and coated her eyes. She blinked, trying to get her bearings and something bumped her from behind.

"Sorry," A stranger said as he maneuvered around her.

"No problem. I—"

"Holly, you need to keep up. Hang onto my mane."

She followed the unfamiliar voice not completely surprised to see a solid white donkey walking just a couple of steps ahead. Holly made up the distance and took the handhold he offered. "Thanks."

"No problem. It seems as if everyone is in a hurry to get somewhere today. You'll get trampled if you aren't careful. I'm Stu, by the way."

"Stu?"

The donkey lowered his head. "It's short for stubborn. I guess you could say it's a donkey thing."

Holly took a second to process his response. Not just the words, but the voice. Stu had an unusually deep voice. More the voice one would expect of a grizzly bear or a gorilla.

If those animals could talk.

She was definitely losing it.

"Can I ask you a nosey question?" Stu asked.

"I guess."

"Why do people always paint donkeys brown?"

Holly looked at the hand that wasn't clutched in the donkey's mane and saw that she still held the bottle of brown paint.

"Aren't they brown?" she asked. "What color would you like?"

The donkey plodded along beside her for a few seconds. "I guess I'm not sure, but could you do me one favor?"

"I suppose."

He gave her a cheeky grin, something she wouldn't have thought possible for a donkey before then. Of course, lots of impossible things were going on in her garage lately, so she didn't flinch.

"You know those fancy horses you see in pictures?" the donkey asked. "The ones with the star on their foreheads? You can paint me any color you choose, but could you give me a star? I always wanted a star." He shook his head, and the bridle rattled. "Nothing big or fancy, mind you. Don't want the other animals in the stable to think I'm putting on airs."

Holly couldn't help but grin. "I can do that." With the next blink Holly was back in the garage, holding the small porcelain animal in her hands. She picked up the brush and began to paint.

"So, what's your part in this story?" Holly asked as she worked.

"I'm the most important animal in the tale," Stu answered. "Without me, the baby Jesus might have been born along the side of the road somewhere."

"Is that so?"

"Without a doubt. I had no idea of the precious cargo I carried on that trip, but something told me to watch where I put my feet on that dirty, pitted road. One misstep could have led to disaster." He turned his head away from Holly so she could reach a difficult spot behind his ear. "Mary was so tired that night, but in spite of that, she was kind to me, patting my neck and whispering encouragement. Why, I'd have carried her to the next town if necessary."

"What made you stop when you did?"

"I always thought that was Joseph's decision, and a strange one at that, seeing as how it was such a dinky place. Hardly any inns at all. But I figured he wanted to be there, something to do with Bethlehem being his ancestral home. Now that I've heard what Melchior told you, about all the ancient prophesies pointing to Bethlehem as the birthplace of the Christ child, it makes way more sense." Stu tossed his head and snorted. "Life would be so much easier for everyone if they'd just share the plan. But no one thinks to tell us donkeys anything. They just load us up and expect us to do as we're told."

Holly pulled the brush back. "Talk all you want, but you have to hold still."

"Sorry." He became still as...well, porcelain. "Anyway, we had just crossed the boundary into Bethlehem when Mary leaned over my neck and groaned. What she said nearly stopped my heart."

"What did she say?"

"Oh, not much. Just three little words that changed history. 'The baby's coming.' *Baby?* I thought. *I've got a baby on board?* We had to stop right there. Joseph had the same idea, but the town was so full of people that we almost didn't find a place to stay. Someone finally took pity on us and pointed us to the stable in their back yard. It wasn't much of a room, but it beat the roadside. I'll never forget the minute that baby was born. Let me tell you, He came out with a healthy set of lungs and an angel choir in the sky." Stu looked at Holly, and she lifted the paintbrush just in time. "That sort of leads to someone else's story. You planning to work on the shepherd soon?"

"Probably. Now hold real still." Holly opened a jar of white paint and dabbed a tiny amount on Stu's forehead. "Perfect." She put the donkey back on the table. "You are quite handsome."

"I want to see, I want to see. Please let me see."

"I'll bring a mirror out next time, but for now, let's get you fired and dry." She set the timer on the kiln and slid the donkey inside.

"Thank you," Stu said, his deep voice echoing in the oven.

"You're welcome." Holly closed the door.

"You're very kind."

She turned at the words and saw the angel watching her with an appreciative smile.

"He wanted a star." She shrugged. "It's a pretty small thing."

"Not to him."

Holly didn't know which was worse. Being scolded by a porcelain figure or being praised by one. Instead of answering she thumbed her phone to life to check the time. It seemed as if the conversation with Stu and the painting had taken a lot of time. In reality just ninety minutes had passed since she'd opened the boxes. She had plenty of time. She studied the shepherd. He wore a simple tunic and sandals. She figured his clothing would have been some sort of rough homespun fabric, or maybe leather. In any case, a lighter brown than the one she'd used on Stu. It wouldn't take much to get an initial coat of paint on.

The persistent angel cleared his throat. "I heard what you said to your sister earlier. Did you mean it?"

The question sent a wave of guilt over Holly. She closed her eyes, tried to isolate the source, and failed. Either she'd mollified Sage with a load of feel-good nonsense, in which case she should feel bad. Or she'd heard and spoken the truth—a truth she flatly refused to believe for herself— in which case, she should feel bad. Whichever it was, she wasn't going to deal with it right then. "Keep talking, and you're going back in the box."

Gabriel crossed his arms, the audible words switched to words in her mind. *I don't need to be out of the box for you to hear me.*

She didn't like the angel's smug smile. An idea occurred to her, and she sprouted her own smile. She opened the drawer on the worktable, pulled out a set of earbuds, and connected them to her phone. In a matter of seconds, she was jamming to her favorite playlist. *I should have thought of this sooner.*

The word *stubborn* filtered through the lyrics as she picked up the shepherd. For an instant, the world blurred around her while the music she'd been so grateful for disappeared.

The next thing she knew she fell hard onto a grassy slope under a sky strewn with more stars than she'd ever seen.

Holly scrambled up, dusting off her jeans as she turned in a small circle. She was surrounded by sheep. Some sleeping. Some waddling about. Some bleating. To her left, a small campfire flicked, surrounded by a half dozen shepherds in quiet conversation.

What in the world?

"Since you don't want to listen, then see." Gabriel's voice resounded in the quiet night.

Suddenly the night sky was split by a brilliant light. The noise of joyful singing filled the air.

Though she couldn't tear her eyes from the sight, she felt and heard the shepherds scrambling to their feet. They stood all around her, all watching what she was watching.

The air filled with booming words as an angel Holly recognized stepped out of the light. The shepherds fell to their knees. Without conscious thought, Holly found herself huddled beside them.

"Fear not: for, behold, I bring you good tidings of great joy, which shall be to all people. For unto you is born this day in the city of David a Savior, which is Christ the Lord. And this shall be a sign unto you; Ye shall find the babe wrapped in swaddling clothes, lying in a manger."

The lights got even brighter. When Holly looked up she couldn't count the angels hovering above the field as they sang.

"Glory to God in the highest, and on earth peace, goodwill toward men."

It was awesome and terrifying. In the next instant the scenery changed, and Holly realized she was in the stable. Mary was there in the maroon robe Holly had painted just a few days before. Joseph stood guard nearby, his attire colorless, as if he wouldn't be real until Holly painted him. Clover chewed her cud in an adjoining stall, and Stu winked at her from his place near the manger. The shepherds crowded around, jostling for position. Holly followed their gazes.

There was a baby in the manger just as the angel had said.

Holly's knees went weak, and she sank to the ground next to the sleeping infant.

"This can't be real," she whispered.

The baby opened His eyes and met her gaze with one filled with infinite wisdom mixed with newborn innocence. Tears gathered as Holly closed her eyes. When she opened them again, she was back in the garage, on her knees, grasping a half-painted shepherd.

~

"THANKS," Riley said as the server left their food and departed. He looked across the table at Holly's plate of street tacos. The salsa on her order was advertised as "Not for the faint-hearted". Indeed, the steam that wafted up from the dish to tease his nose carried more than a hint of spice. Time would tell if Holly was brave or foolhardy.

"Everything look OK?"

"Yeah, it looks great." She picked up the cup of salsa and held it across the table. "Last chance to give it a try."

Riley looked at the chili relleno lying harmlessly on his plate. He appreciated the word *harmless* when it applied to his food. "Thanks, I'll pass."

"Suit yourself."

He watched in horror as Holly poured the salsa over the tacos. "You aren't going to taste it on a chip or something first? What if its more than you bargained for?"

"Taste testing is for wimps."

"Yeah, OK. But"—he held his hand across the table—"we should probably bless this just to be safe."

Holly snorted at his joke, but she didn't hesitate to take his hand and bow her head.

Riley spared a second to wonder about the subtle change he'd noticed in Holly this evening. He couldn't put his finger on it, but something seemed different. Subdued might be a better word.

That she'd agreed to the blessing without a sneer gave him hope that her heart was softening.

"Jesus, thank you for the food we are about to eat. Bless it to our bodies and our bodies to Your service." He paused and cracked an eye open to look at Holly's plate a final time. "Protect our stomachs, Father. Some of us are going to need it. Amen."

Holly gave his hand a quick smack before she reached for a taco. "Goof." She locked her gaze on his and took a healthy bite.

Riley pressed his lips together when, two seconds later, Holly's eyes went round and tears gathered in the corners. The tip of her nose turned red, and tiny beads of sweat broke out on her upper lip. She swallowed and grabbed for her glass of soda. He couldn't tell if she was breathing. He looked around for a waiter, but before he could raise his hand in summons, Holly set the glass down and gasped.

"Wow."

"Too much? Do you need to order something else?"

"Are you kidding? This stuff is amazing. I may need an additional serving." Holly took a second bite as if to prove her point. She lifted her napkin from her lap and dabbed at her mouth. "Do I have food...?" She motioned to her mouth. "I can't feel my lips."

"You are... I don't have a word for what you are." He laughed. "But as long as you enjoy it, who am I to judge?" He cut into his own dinner and took a bite of the poblano pepper filled with melted cheese and savory carne asada. He couldn't remember when or where he'd had better food or company.

It didn't take long for them to exhaust the details of their day. Riley provided a quick update on the progress of the shelves for Ember's store, and Holly told him about the book she was reading. Before their entrees were half-finished, silence hung over the table.

She was so stunning. Her auburn curls hung around her face in the most distracting way. He longed to gather them in his hands to see if they were as soft as they looked. His gaze flicked to her mouth, and he wondered what it would be like to taste those lips?

Would they be soft and sweet or hot and spicy? Considering what she was eating, he'd guess the second.

With a conscious effort, he jerked his eyes back to his plate as he waged a silent battle with his emotions. He was a minister, and she wasn't a believer. God wanted him to offer her help, not romance.

Jesus, I could use a little help of my own. Show me what she needs, but guard my heart.

"So why the food bank?" Holly asked.

The unexpected question caught Riley off guard. He replayed the last few seconds of their dinner to make sure he hadn't missed something while he was begging God for help.

"I can tell you, but it will touch on some of the issues you said you were tired of hearing about."

"That's fine. I think I need to hear the story."

Riley studied her face for a second. Was she serious? He was happy that he hadn't been wrong about the shift in her attitude, but...*Father?*

Be honest with her.

Riley sipped his tea while he considered the best place to start. When he leaned forward, she matched his pose.

"It's really more about the ministry than the food bank," he said. "I want to be a full-time pastor someday. That means I have a lot to learn when it comes to service and working with people. The ministry is like any other job. You start at the bottom and work your way up." Riley floundered at his own words. "Sorry, I didn't mean to make my work at the center seem less important than it is. I believe in what I'm doing. Nothing is as important to me as doing what God called me to do. But as a young minister looking at a life-long career path, this first job is just a stepping stone to where I hope to be someday." He put his head in his hands. "And that still sounds incredibly arrogant."

"Not at all," Holly said. "I get what you're trying to say. So let me change my question. Why the ministry?"

"That's a much easier answer. For me, the ministry is all about truth."

Holly raised her brows.

"Do you remember what I said about my father when we were talking the other day?" Riley asked.

"Yes."

"I won't go into the whole story, but I'll tell you that I was raised in a very strict *religious* cult called The Body. You'll notice that I said religious, *not* Christian."

"There's a difference?"

"More than a little," Riley assured her. "You can be religious about brushing your teeth, but good oral hygiene won't get you into heaven. When Dad died and Mom moved us to Garfield, it didn't take either of us long to see the difference. The Bible that The Body taught was as far from the truth as black is from white. Complete male domination. Arranged marriages, women confined to the community. They were allowed no entertainment, no jobs, nothing but basic schooling and were taught that a woman's only way to heaven was through total subservience to her husband."

Holly rolled her eyes. "Even I know that's bull."

"Exactly. Once I heard the truth, once I accepted it, once I saw the damage being done by such false teachings, I knew I wanted to dedicate my future to truth. The day God called me into the ministry was the happiest day of my life."

Riley nudged his plate aside and held his hand out. Holly placed hers in his. "I know you don't want to be preached to. That's not what I'm trying to do, but you've been raised with a couple of lies...just like I was. I'd love it if you'd give me the chance to show you the truth."

Holly looked down at their joined hands and back to his face. "Like...what lies?"

"The food bank thing, for one." He told her about his latest experience with her father. "You were right about him. I got just a small sample of what you lived with your whole life. It was a wake-up call for me."

"I'm sorry," she whispered. When she tried to pull her hand away, Riley held fast.

"Why are you apologizing? You didn't do anything wrong. Now I understand why you see centers like mine as a crutch, something that can cause more harm than good where some people are concerned. But even knowing what I know now, I have to tell you that that's a lie. There's a whole other side to what we do that you've never seen. If you can come to the center some afternoon, I'll show you the positives."

Holly's expression told him that she wasn't convinced. "What's the other thing?"

Riley met her gaze. He knew there were tears in his eyes, and he didn't care. If he never spoke another word to her, he had to make her understand this one thing. "Holly, you were never taught about a Jesus who loves you, so you just assume that He doesn't. That lie is just as dangerous to you as the false teachings of The Body were to me. Come to church with me in the morning. Let me start to show you the truth."

Holly stared at him for so long that he was sure she was going to say no. When she finally nodded her head, it was all he could do to keep from shouting for joy.

CHAPTER SEVENTEEN

When her alarm went off on Sunday morning, Holly's first inclination was to bounce it across the room. Instead she cracked one eye open and looked at the time. Riley was picking her up in a little while. For church.

Why, why, why had she agreed to this?

You know why.

Did she? Holly closed her eyes and drew Riley's sweet, earnest face into her memory. Sweet? That hardly described it, but that word would have to do until she'd had enough coffee, and time, to come up with the male equivalent to *drop-dead gorgeous*. But that wasn't why she'd agreed to church.

It was obvious that he liked her more than a little. Holly was used to Sage getting the attention. Sage, with her flawless complexion, perfect features, and a fiery personality that matched her red hair, was the eye candy most men gravitated to. So Holly was a little flattered by the attention of such a sexy guy. But that wasn't it either.

Holly laid her hand against her cheek and felt the skin beneath her fingers tingle in memory. When he'd walked her to the door last night, she'd been sure he was going to kiss her. There were no words to explain how much she'd wanted him to. But after several seconds of fiddling with her keys, an open invitation, according to an old Will Smith movie, Riley had simply taken them from her hands, opened the door for her, and kissed her cheek before nudging her across the threshold and pulling the door closed between them. His quiet "lock up" had filtered through the door seconds before his car started. She added considerate and polite to sweet, gorgeous, and sexy and still didn't have an answer for why she'd agreed to attend church this morning.

You know why. The pesky little internal voice persisted. Why did the voice of her conscience sound like Gabriel these days?

Yep...she did. It had been the tears she'd seen in his eyes. She hadn't seen a guy cry since she'd beaned Timmy Calder in the head with a wild pitch the summer before fifth grade. Timmy had fallen to home plate kicking, screaming, and bawling. Not a single tear had escaped the corners of Riley's eyes last night, but what Riley lacked in theatrics was more than made up for in sincerity.

Holly could count on the fingers of one hand the people who had ever shed a tear on her behalf. Nana. Sage. "Now, make that three," she whispered as she added Riley to the list. He believed in what he said, and he cared enough about her to let the emotion show.

And that had done it.

If Riley could put aside all the macho trappings of his species, then surely Holly could give him one shot to prove his point. Maybe it would get that fool Nativity set off her back as well. She hadn't thought of that last night, but it was a definite mark in the plus column.

She tossed the covers aside, shrugged out of her pajamas, and opened her closet. What did one wear to church? Holly pulled out a pretty linen dress in moss green and held it up to the mirror. Green was her favorite color, and the dress really brought out the color of her eyes and complimented her auburn hair, but it might be too dressy...or not dressy enough. She chewed on her lip and took out a pair of comfortable jeans and a navy turtleneck. Definitely conservative, but... After a few seconds of consideration, she replaced the turtleneck and dug out a filmy, pale blue peasant blouse with flowers embroidered around the ruched neckline. The attached cami kept the sheer fabric of the blouse from being too revealing, and she liked the color almost as much as the green. She waffled between her choices.

Dressed in her bra and panties, Holly scooted across the hall and knocked on Sage's door. "You awake?"

The door swung open. Sage was still dressed in a long T-shirt bearing their high school logo. "Barely. What's up?"

"I need to know which outfit is good for church this morning." She lifted the options, but Sage said nothing.

The question hung in the air for longer than it should have while the expression on Sage's face went from sleepy to shocked to relieved to deliberation in the space of a breath. Holly braced for the boatload of questions that she knew she'd just invited and breathed a sigh of gratitude when Sage held her peace, throttled the look on her face back to neutral, and studied the outfits.

"They're both nice." She tilted her head. "You going with Riley?"

"Yes. I thought maybe the dress, but then I thought jeans, but...church."

"You're overthinking. Either choice is fine, so wear what makes you comfortable."

"Lot of help you are." The words were a frustrated mutter as Holly turned back to her own room.

Sage's laughter filled the hallway. "Wear the dress. It's a beautiful color on you, and Riley will love it."

Holly turned back to face her sister. "You think so?"

"I know so. You know..." Sage held up a finger. "Give me a second." She ducked back into her room and returned a moment later, a pair of gold-tone sandals dangling from her fingers. "Try these, since I messed up your shoe shopping yesterday."

Holly took the shoes and studied Sage's face. She'd almost forgotten how upset Sage had been yesterday. This morning it was good to see the familiar peace return to her features. "Are you OK?

You were still in your room when I left yesterday, and you were gone when I got home from dinner."

"It's all good." She placed her hands on Holly's shoulders, turned her, and nudged toward her own room. "Go have fun with Riley, keep an open mind, and learn things. You might be surprised to find out just how much fun church can be."

Two hours later, Riley parked his car in Calvary Worship Church's huge lot, circled the car, and took Holly's hand to help her out. He drew her hand through the bend of his arm and squeezed her fingers.

"Your hands are like ice," he said, looking up at the cloudless blue sky. "Are you cold?"

"Not particularly." Holly looked at the gigantic church surrounded by a half dozen smaller buildings. *Did her feet count?* She took a breath. "It's just a little strange." Her free hand swept in a wide arch. "Everything's fully insured, right?"

Riley frowned down at her. "I suppose. Why?"

"Just, when the roof collapses..."

Riley turned her to face him and wrapped her in his arms, his body shaking with laughter. "It's going to be fine. I promise." He released her and took a step back. "Did I tell you how amazing you look in that dress and how lucky I am to have you by my side this morning?"

Holly smiled as the warmth of his words melted some of the ice in her veins. "You mentioned it."

Riley started forward once more. "Just making sure. 'Cause when we get inside and all the other single guys start trying to hog your attention, I want you to remember who saw you first."

Riley needn't have worried. The introvert in Holly kept her close to his side as he led her to a seat. He waved and nodded to a couple of people while she took in the crowd. Sage had been right about her outfit. Either one would have been fine. The clothing choices of the women in the congregation ran from senior women dressed in beaded jackets, skirts, and heels, to teens wearing T-shirts, frayed jeans, and flip flops. That her sleeveless summer dress fell squarely in the middle of those two extremes had her confidence ratcheting up a notch or two.

As for the service, she stood when Riley stood and sat when Riley sat. The up-tempo music presented by the praise and worship team had her tapping her feet to songs she didn't know the words to. She even found herself clapping to the beat a time or two as the people surrounding her joined in enthusiastically.

The atmosphere in the room changed when an energetic middle-aged man dressed in slacks and a black pullover came to stand at the front of the room. As the last note of music faded, his face lit with a smile, and his voice boomed over the PA system.

"Happy Sunday morning, Church. What a glorious day to be in the house of God. For any visitors I haven't met yet, I'm Pastor Hodges, and I want to thank you for choosing to worship with us today."

Excitement rose off the man like carbonated bubbles in a freshly poured soda. Holly found herself infected by the shift in the atmosphere. She leaned forward as he stepped behind a podium and opened his Bible. "I want to dive right into the word today. We're going to talk about purpose. If you want to follow along, my text is found in Jeremiah, chapter one verse five. I'm reading from the King James Version. This is God speaking to Jeremiah. 'Before I formed thee in the belly I knew thee: and before thou camest out of the womb I sanctified thee, and ordained thee a prophet unto the nations.'"

Holly leaned forward when she recognized Ruthie's words from a few days before. For the next thirty minutes, Holly sat, enthralled, as the pastor told them about Jeremiah and God's purpose in his life. "Now don't get me wrong. God has not called everyone in this building to be a minister. But sometimes I think people believe that if they are not called to the ministry, then they are not called. That couldn't be further from the truth. He has called each of us to do something. Not a single one of us was born without a purpose, a purpose we need to spend time praying about, looking for, and preparing for." He clasped his hands behind his back and stepped down from the platform, continuing the sermon as he walked nearer the congregation.

"It doesn't have to be a spiritual gifting to qualify, and it won't always be glamorous. Jeremiah was doing exactly what God called him to do, and he spent time in an abandoned well up to his armpits in slime. The world needs ministers and pastors, but we need doctors, teachers, and hairdressers as well. We also need garbage men, plumbers, and moms willing to change dirty diapers. And let me share this with you. Whatever God's plan for your life, I can promise you that you will never be completely happy in this world until you find it.

"As the praise team comes back, I want you to think about what I've said today. Are you looking for your purpose? Do you know what God created you to do?"

His eyes roamed the crowd, and Holly could have sworn that his look lingered on her for a second. Why did she feel as if he was speaking directly to her?

~

Holly still didn't have the answer to her question hours later when she wandered out to the garage. What had the preacher meant? What was this invisible purpose that everyone except her seemed so convinced of? She still wasn't sure that believing in a God directed purpose for her life would make things better. She worked hard. Her life was good just the way it was.

She turned the kiln on, intending to add small details to each of the characters so that they could all cure overnight. Even with all the distractions of the last two weeks the project was coming together much quicker than she'd originally imagined. The angel and Mary were complete. Once she finished the shepherd's sandals, she could pack him away. Melchior's turban and the gift he carried still needed some work, and Stu and Clover's hoofs and tails awaited finishing touches.

"He was a tool."

Holly looked up from the rack of paints she was perusing to find Gabriel watching her from the center of the table.

"What?"

"You were wondering about the pastor's words this morning. He was a tool. When God needed to reprimand a wayward prophet, He used a donkey. When God needed to redirect Jonah, He used a fish. When God needed to feed Elijah during a drought, He used a raven and a widow. When God needed to speak to Holly Hoffman, He used a Nativity set and a minister who wouldn't know you from Eve." Gabriel's wings fluttered when his shoulders lifted in a shrug. "When God wants to reach out to one of His children, His pursuit is both loving and relentless. We are all just tools in the Father's hands. He won't circumvent your free will, but He won't be ignored either."

Holly didn't know what to say to that, so she said nothing. She finished selecting the paints she needed and made quick work of the remaining bits and pieces of the nearly finished characters. She fully expected the angel to keep prodding her, but for once he fell silent and allowed her to work in peace.

One by one, she placed the finished pieces in the oven and sealed the door, then turned to look at the remaining figurines. Joseph and the baby Jesus. Her hand hovered in indecision for a split second before she picked up Joseph. That baby might look innocent and harmless, but the last few days had proved just how deceiving looks could be. She lifted Joseph to eye level and contemplated where to begin.

"Thank you," he said before she had time to reach for a brush.

No longer surprised at their ability to speak, Holly grinned at the robed man. "I haven't done anything yet."

"But you have." Joseph swept his hand in Mary's direction. "I love seeing Mary in that rich color. I worked hard to provide for my family, and we were blessed. We always had a roof over our heads and food on the table. But I was never able to give Mary all the little extras I thought she deserved. The babies just came too fast."

"You did fine," Mary said.

"You're beautiful," Joseph told his wife.

Holly was amused to see Mary's cheeks turn pink with a color she'd not applied.

"Isn't she beautiful?" Joseph asked as he turned back to Holly. "It was love at first sight for me."

"Really?" Holly picked up a brush and applied the first swipe of the deep forest green paint she'd selected.

"Yes," Joseph answered. "Ours, like most others in our time, was an arranged marriage. Back then, you did as you were told, married who you were told, and if you were lucky, you ended up with mutual respect. But Mary? He shook his head, a small smile playing at the corner of his lips. The first time I saw her, she just took my breath away."

Holly heard the words, though her concentration was focused as she painted the folds of his robe where they bunched around his arm. "So, the whole pregnancy thing didn't bother you?"

The little porcelain figurine lowered his head. "Well, I'll admit that my initial reaction was less than ideal. A baby? I knew it wasn't mine, and even though I'd heard the prophecies my whole life, I had more than a little trouble accepting the whole angel story."

Gabriel fluttered his wings in response to Joseph's words.

Joseph gave the angel a reverent nod. "But I loved her, and I didn't want her disgraced. I decided to send her away."

"Seems reasonable."

"I thought so until I tried to go to sleep that night."

"Guilt?" Holly asked.

"No. Angel. You and Mary aren't the only ones to entertain a heavenly visitor. That night, an angel came to me and verified everything that Mary had told me. Even then, I still had lingering doubts."

Holly stopped painting and waited.

Joseph raised his hands. "Yeah, I mean me, a carpenter, raising God's son? That's pretty intimidating. But then, I had a moment of insight."

"And that was?"

"That Mary wasn't the only one chosen. God's son would need a strong earthly father to keep Jesus safe and teach him the things he needed to know. Out of all the men in the world, He chose me. I guess I could have refused, but I know enough about God's purpose in our lives to believe that if I had taken another path, I would never have been happy. You and I have that in common."

Holly's focus shifted to the face of the little figurine. "How do you mean?"

His eyes were fixed on hers. "God had a plan for my life from the day I was born," Joseph said. "He has a plan for you as well."

CHAPTER EIGHTEEN

"Enough."

The single word was an angry hiss accompanied by the sound of her cup hitting the table with an irritated thunk. The force of the blow opened a small tear near the base of the paper cup, and Holly watched as liquid oozed on to the Formica surface. She grabbed a handful of napkins from the dispenser and used them to sop up the mess.

"See what you made me do?"

Holly pressed her lips together and bowed her head over the table in the McDonald's dining room on Friday afternoon. A quick study from under her lashes revealed that none of the occupants seated around her seemed to be paying any attention to the crazy woman sitting in the corner booth talking to herself. She propped both elbows on the table, put her head in her hands, and threaded her fingers through her hair. Was it possible to have a stomachache in your head? An unsettled feeling where things kept churning around and around, looking for a way out?

God has a plan for your life.

There it was again.

Holly closed her eyes, not sure if she was going to laugh or cry. So far, her week had been packed as full as she could make it. She'd cleaned ten houses, walked more dogs than she cared to count, and bagged, tagged, and delivered her largest ever Avon order. Each night she'd fallen into bed exhausted, using fatigue as an excuse to ignore the work that waited for her in the garage.

How's that working for you?

"Shut up!" She gave her hair a tug, took a deep breath, and straightened in her seat. She had to get a grip. Every time she got still, every time she took a breath, every time she closed her eyes and tried to sleep, Joseph's words cycled over and over in her mind.

God has a plan for your life.

A plan for her? That was almost funny. When did that plan start? When she'd been born to parents who'd never wanted her? When the only adult who'd ever loved her died while those parents slept off their latest high? Maybe it was when Gilbert and Cindy packed up and left their daughters to fend for themselves. Not, she reminded herself, that fending for themselves was anything new.

Holly gathered up her trash. What her life had been before didn't matter. She was in a good place now, and now was what counted. But the *now* was hers, earned through hard work and determination. As far as she could see, God hadn't been involved in the before or the after. He had a universe to run. Surely He had better things to do than concern Himself with the life and times of Holly Hoffman.

When her phone rang, she grabbed it, grateful for the distraction but troubled about her afternoon obligation at the same time. She could always back out. With the week she'd had, claiming she didn't feel well wouldn't be a lie, but a promise was a promise.

"Hey, Riley."

"Hey back," Riley said. "Are we good?"

Holly dropped her trash in the can by the door and pushed her way outside. "As a matter of fact we are. I have the whole afternoon free."

"And you're sure you want to do this? Not that I'd try to talk you out of it, but I don't want you to feel pressured."

Holly thought back to her Sunday lunch with Riley and his

second invitation to visit the food bank. He wanted her to see the work they did from an adult perspective in the hopes of dispelling some of her childhood biases. She didn't know if that was possible, but if her choices were spending the afternoon with Riley or working on the Nativity set, Riley won.

She clicked open the locks of the Jeep and scooted inside. "You're not pressuring me. I told you I'd stop by."

"I know, but you don't sound like yourself. You sound sort of...tired."

Holly almost laughed at his words. Tired was one way to put it. She wondered how he'd react if she told him that his Nativity set was driving her a little crazier every day and stealing more and more of her sleep every night. She leaned back against the headrest and gave herself a moment. That wasn't a conversation she intended to have with anyone.

"I'd be lying if I said the week hadn't been twelve days long already, but, I'm looking forward to seeing you."

"You just made me the happiest person in the building," Riley said. "I promise I won't work you too hard, and if something comes up and you need to leave before five, just say so."

"OK, see you in about ten minutes." Holly closed the call, buckled her seatbelt, and started the Jeep. Despite her words, a sense of dread had her hesitating to pull out of the parking lot. She closed her eyes and worked to swallow past the lump in her throat while a knot of anxiety grew in her stomach like an out-of-control snowball. *Breathe. It's four hours, and you can leave whenever you want. You are in control of this visit, not Gilbert and Cindy. Give yourself a chance.*

The pressure eased. She could do this. She *would* do this. With her jaw set, she put the Jeep in gear and pointed it in the direction of the food bank. Riley was waiting for her when she pulled into the crowded lot. His welcoming smile sent a zip of electricity down her spine. He really was just the most gorgeous guy she'd ever met, and he wanted her to respect and understand what he was doing.

Some feeling she couldn't identify welled up inside of her, bringing with it a desire to do just that.

She waved and pulled into the closest parking space. Riley had her door open before she killed the engine. He bowed and swept a hand in the direction of the building.

"Welcome to my humble establishment." When he straightened, he took her hand and helped her from the Jeep.

"Wow, do you treat all your volunteers with such chivalry?"

"Only the special ones." Riley led her past the line of customers and into the building. He must have felt the tremor that ran through her body because he squeezed her fingers. "You sure you're OK?"

"Just nerves. You're sure *they* won't show up here today?"

Riley obviously didn't need an explanation of who *they* were. "Like I told you Sunday. Our clients are only allowed to visit once a month. They aren't eligible to shop again for a couple of weeks. Gilbert tried to see me earlier in the week, but I had the receptionist shoo him away. He needs to follow the rules just like all the other clients."

Holly wasn't a hundred percent sold by his reassurances, but she was here. Leaving now would be just one more thing Gilbert and Cindy took from her. She was done with that. "What do you need me to do?"

Riley released her and rubbed his hands together. "You don't know it yet, but your presence here is a godsend. Can you run a computer? Are you good with Excel?"

"I won't be overseeing any NASA rocket launches, but I can manage. Why?"

Riley led her to a desk in the corner of the room. "We were already shorthanded today thanks to the flu bug, but that just got worse. The lady who does check-in got a call during lunch. Looks like her daughter broke her arm on the playground." He handed her into a chair, jiggled the mouse, and typed in a password when the screen came to life. An Excel sheet popped up.

"It's pretty easy. You just ask the client for their name. Find them on the list—it's alphabetical—and verify the date next to their name. If the date is today or earlier, they can shop today." He wrote a date on the notepad next to the computer. "Overwrite the old date with this one." He tapped a stack of cards. "Print their next shopping date on one of these, give it to them, and send them to the waiting area. If anyone comes in who isn't in the system, or if anyone is ineligible to shop today, or if anyone gives you a hard time, send them in to talk to me. Questions?"

Holly took a second to look at the spreadsheet and process Riley's instructions. She held the firm opinion that with a reliable internet connection and a decent spreadsheet program a person could manage just about anything. "I think I've got it."

Riley squeezed her shoulder. "You're the best. If you need anything"—he pointed to the door behind her and to the left —"that's my office. You dig me out of this mess today, and dinner is on me once we close."

"Deal." Holly shooed him back to his office, took a deep breath, and smiled at the first person in line. "Can I have your name please?"

The next few hours sped by without complication. Holly got into a rhythm with the clients and the computer and had the check-in process running smoothly. She sent a couple off to wait in the chairs adjacent to the shopping area, made the update in the computer, and looked up to find an empty line for the first time since she'd sat down. A glance at the clock in the corner of the monitor put a smile on her face. The center closed in ten minutes.

She'd done it. Holly couldn't say that anything in her mindset had changed, but the afternoon had been better than she'd expected.

The door opened, and a young woman came to stand at the desk. A little girl—Holly guessed her to be about six—clung to the woman's jacket with one hand and clutched a bedraggled baby doll with the other. The woman's gaze shifted nervously from object to object, landing everywhere but on Holly.

"Could I get your name?" Holly asked.

"Christy Baker."

Holly bent to her computer, but she couldn't help but hear the small whine that issued from the little girl.

The woman put an arm around the child. "Not much longer, I promise."

Holly went through the Bs on the spreadsheet a second time before looking up. "I'm sorry. I'm not finding your name."

Christy Baker finally met Holly's gaze. "Oh, I won't be in your system. We're new in town. Can you tell me how to get enrolled in the program?"

Holly scooted her chair back, intending to get Riley. "I can't, but—"

"Mama said you'd be able to get us some food." The little girl flashed a gap-toothed smile. "She said if I was really good, there might be cookies. I haven't had a cookie in a long time, so I'm trying to be extra good."

The woman ran a hand through the little girl's wispy brown hair and bent down to her level. "Shh, Darla. Let Mama talk to the lady."

Holly watched as tears gathered in Darla's green eyes. "But you promised." Her voice was tiny and shaky. "I'm trying to be good, but I'm hungry."

The woman closed her eyes and blew out a breath that shuddered with emotion. "I know, baby, I'm doing my best." When she stood again and looked at Holly, Christy's eyes swam with unshed tears. "Please, is there anything you can do to help us? My baby hasn't eaten since yesterday. Anything is better than nothing. Just don't send us away."

Holly swallowed hard as her own tears gathered. How many times had she stood under the gaze of a stranger, hungry and afraid? Something pounded in her chest and threatened to overwhelm her. She'd grown to resent those strangers and the power they seemed to wield over her, but she couldn't remember a single time when she'd gone away hungry.

For all the bitterness of her past and her jaded view of this system, she never would have considered herself cold or heartless. Looking at Darla, Holly had no idea if her mother's claims were honest. She didn't really care. Right now she was ready to march into the shopping area and find the biggest package of cookies she could get her hands on. Forget that. She'd get their address, go to Walmart, and buy out the whole cookie aisle, even if it took all of her savings.

Was this what all those people had felt for her and Sage for all those years? A desire to help that overrode any judgment, any preconceived notion of who deserved what? It didn't matter if Christy's story was honest or not. It didn't matter where she was from or what she might do tomorrow. All that mattered was a hungry little girl who wanted a cookie.

"Give me a second." Her voice was so full of emotion that Holly barely recognized it as her own. She bolted into Riley's office, closed the door, leaned against it, and let the tears come.

"Holly?" Riley hurried across the office and took her into his arms. "What is it? Is Gilbert out there?"

Holly could barely speak. She motioned. "No, but there's a little girl out there. You have to help. Please tell me you have a plan to help."

Riley backed her into a chair. "Sit right here. I'll be back."

Holly folded her arms around herself and nodded, unable to get another word around the tears that clogged her throat. Riley was a good guy. He'd see to it that Darla got what she needed.

Suddenly, Holly's tears became great gasping sobs as years of bitterness broke through a dam of self-pity and loathing. She couldn't help a single day of her childhood, but she could decide—would decide from this day forward—what she allowed her past to make of her.

God has a plan for your life.

Holly bit her lip. Maybe that idea wasn't so farfetched after all.

When Riley came back into the office, Holly was still in the chair. He stooped down in front of her and took her hands in his. "Are you going to be OK?"

"You helped them, right?"

"Yes, ma'am. We sent them on their way with an emergency ration box and instructions to come back tomorrow with proof of residency so that we can get them set up in the system."

Holly's chin trembled. "All that baby wanted was a cookie."

"I put a package in the box."

Holly leaned her forehead against Riley's. The contact drained a bit more of the tension away. "You're a good man." She swallowed. "And"—her voice broke as another sob escaped—"you're doing important work."

Riley leaned back on his heels. "Thanks...?" The uptick at the end of the word turned it into a question.

Holly nodded. "You heard me."

Riley's frown was a bit confused. "Wow...that was fast. I mean...I hoped to make an impression on you. I didn't think it would happen on your first visit."

"Neither did I." She glanced away before her gaze came back to his. "Would it hurt your feelings if I took a raincheck on dinner? I've got some things I need to think about. We probably need to talk about some of that, but—"

"I get it." Riley pulled her to her feet. "Call me when you're ready to talk."

CHAPTER NINETEEN

Holly drove home in an October thunderstorm that lashed at the trees and threw buckets of water at the Jeep. She pulled into the driveway, shifted into park, and leaned back in the seat. She stared out the windshield, not looking at anything in particular, just...thinking, waiting for a break in the rain, lulled by the sound and motion of the wipers.

She'd had some preconceived ideas about how this day would end. Nowhere in those thoughts had she imagined herself as anything but grateful it was over. Her visit to the food bank was supposed to be something she checked off her obligation list for the week. A one-and-done sort of thing that, if she were honest, was more about earning some brownie points with Riley—a guy she liked probably more than she should—than being helpful to his cause.

Mission accomplished.

"Yeah." Holly's whispered acknowledgment filled the car as she rubbed the achy spot behind her rib cage. That, and a huge crack in the armor around her heart that left her vulnerable. What was she supposed to do with that? Could she repair it? Did she want to?

Thunk...thunk...thunk...

The swish of the wipers, which she'd found soothing a few seconds earlier, suddenly grated on her nerves. She reached out to turn the wipers off, and her hand brushed against the purple beaded bracelet she'd wrangled out of Maggie several weeks ago. Holly'd hung it on the wiper lever the morning she'd bought it to keep from damaging it while she worked. It'd been hanging there ever since, forgotten each time she went into the house. Holly slipped it over her hand, turned the car off, and peered at the thick, black clouds through the curtain of rain. The storm didn't look like it was going to pass any time soon. A flash of blinding light followed by an ear-cracking burst of thunder served to put an exclamation point on her thoughts. The rain intensified as the rumbling faded, followed by tiny pings as pea-sized hail bounced off the hood of the Jeep. The twenty-five feet to the front door became a waterlogged hazard. These were the days she regretted the necessity of using their garage for a workspace.

Oh, whaa, whaa, whaa. She needed to get inside before the hail got any bigger.

Holly reached into the back seat and sifted through assorted cleaning supplies, Avon books, and boxes of dog treats. She found what she was looking for, opened the door, popped the umbrella open, grabbed her bag, and made a mad dash to the safety of the porch. The wind made the umbrella almost useless, and her clothes were soaked by the time she stepped under the sloping roof.

Sage came out of the house just as Holly cleared the steps. She tossed a dishtowel in Holly's direction. "I wondered how long you were going to sit out there."

Holly dried her face and blotted the ends of her hair. "Gotta love fall in Oklahoma."

"Yeah, tornado season, part two," Sage said, looking over her sister's shoulder at the puddles forming in the yard. "The power was off for about ten minutes, but it's back on now. Channel nine says the worst of it will be out of here in an hour or so."

"Good. I need to work later, and I can't paint by candlelight." Holly dried her arms and yelped when the elastic bracelet pulled at the tiny hairs on her wrist. She yanked it free and handed it to Sage. "Here. Maggie brought a load of new stuff in the other day. I talked her out of this one. I thought you'd like it."

Sage followed Holly into the house and paused in the entry to examine the gift. Holly's shoulders received a quick squeeze. "I love it. She does such beautiful work." Sage plopped onto the couch, sliding the bracelet onto her wrist. The brocade cushions were littered with paint color cards, a carpet sample board, and fabric swatches. She shoved it all out of the way and made room for Holly. "Speaking of good work, I was out in the garage earlier. You're doing a great job on that Nativity set. The characters are so lifelike, I could almost hear them talking to me."

"Did they...?" Holly's words trailed off as Sage looked at her askance. She sank down on the sofa, bowed her head, and let her hair curtain her face to hide the furious blush that spread across her cheeks.

"Did they what?"

Holly waved the question away. The embarrassment of the moment, her emotional encounter at the food bank, and the constant bombardment of a religious message she wasn't ready to accept gathered in her stomach as if she'd swallowed a piece of lead. She felt the couch shift as Sage leaned forward.

"Holly, are you OK?"

Holly wanted to shrug the question away but found she couldn't. "I don't know. I really don't know anymore." Suddenly she needed answers more than she needed her next breath. "How did you do it?"

"Do what?" Sage's question rang with confusion.

Holly looked up. There were tears hovering in the corners of her eyes, but she didn't care. "How did you turn your life around so easily? How did you embrace all this stuff we were never taught? What made you so willing to forgive Gilbert and Cindy for years of abuse without even being asked?" She swallowed and continued in a shaky voice. "Six months ago, if someone had asked me who was the best and kindest person I knew, I would have pointed to you.

But as good as you were, you're better now in ways I can't even explain."

Holly reached out to Sage and turned her sister's face into the light coming from the lamp. She searched Sage's eyes. "There's something in your eyes that was never there before, some weird peacefulness or something." Her words faltered to a stop when Sage smiled. "I can't explain it." She released Sage's chin and bowed her head a second time. "I think I'm losing my mind."

Sage took Holly's hands and pulled them into her lap. "Do you really want answers to your questions?"

Holly nodded.

"Jesus." Sage didn't continue until Holly looked up. "We lived our whole lives without love. Always feeling like we were in the way, always feeling like we'd done something wrong. Surely the way Gilbert and Cindy treated us had to be our fault, right?" Her voice cracked, and she pressed her lips together for a few seconds as if battling words she was hesitant to speak out loud.

"If we were better, smarter, prettier, maybe they'd love us the way we needed. When I met Jesus, the first thing He said to me—"

"He talked to you?" Holly asked, her mind going to the baby in the manger out in the garage.

"I think He must talk to everyone at some point. And the first thing He said to me was that it wasn't my fault. He wanted me to know that I didn't have to change a thing for Him to love me. He loved me just like I was...bumps, bruises, and all. I had a hard time believing that. There are days when I still do. But I knew that if there was that kind of love out there, I wanted it. I needed it."

Did that kind of love really exist? It was a nice thought, and Sage sounded so sure of herself, but—

"And you know what?" Sage asked.

"What?" Holly's response was barely more than a whisper.

"The more I listened, the more I opened up, the more love I felt. It hasn't been as easy as you think. We both know I've done some pretty horrible things, and from my reaction on Saturday, I've got a long way to go, but every day I wake up, and He still loves me."

Now that the subject Holly'd avoided for so many weeks was out there, open between them, she had so many questions. The one that seemed most urgent, the one that niggled at her fears the most, came out of her mouth. "How can you be sure?"

"The only person I can be sure for is me. You're never going to know until you experience it for yourself. I've been praying for weeks that Jesus would do something so spectacular in your life that you'd know it was Him. That you'd know He loves you."

Holly hesitated with her hand on the doorknob as little goosebumps popped out on her arms. She could admit it to no one but herself, but that tiny baby in the manger scared her more than all the other figurines combined. More than fluttering angel wings and smirking donkeys and big-eyed cows that put words in her head. More even than all those angels lighting up the night sky and singing.

As hard as she was trying to hang onto her unbelief, it seemed to be burning off as if the heat from the kiln were firing *her*.

These people were so real, their story so cohesive, that she'd found her armor deeply dented in more than one place.

I've been praying for weeks that Jesus would do something so spectacular in your life that you'd know He loves you.

Sage's words echoed in Holly's ears. At least now she knew who to blame for this whole thing. It sort of served Sage right that Holly would never be able to share this experience with her in a way she could appreciate.

Much as she'd love to avoid this, she couldn't. She wouldn't, not anymore. Holly acknowledged the words with a determined lift of her chin. She opened the door, stepped into the garage, and sucked in a deep breath to prepare for the encounter to come.

She coughed. Something odd hung in the air.

Holly went straight to the trashcan in the corner. The garbage had been collected two days ago, but they must have missed something. She lifted the lid, but the can was empty. With her nose raised, she sniffed to try to locate the source. The odor was fainter now and seemed to be dissipating rapidly.

Maybe she was still stalling, her nose playing tricks on her.

She approached the table, giving it a wide, cautious berth. The whole set was complete, painted and glazed except for this one last piece. It was her work, but Holly agreed with Sage's assessment. It really was some of her best. Surprising when she considered all the interruptions and weirdness of the last few weeks.

Holly circled the table. Tonight all the figurines were still as statues except for Mary. The little mother had her back to the rest, and she was rocking slightly while a faint humming filled the air. Holly moved to face her, and Mary looked up with a contented smile while she patted the back of the baby nestled against her shoulder.

"I thought you might come tonight, but I wasn't sure," she whispered. A small noise escaped the baby, and Mary cooed, "You're such a good boy." She bundled the baby closer and inhaled. "You know, I had seven babies, and I never got tired of that new baby smell." She tilted her head back a little to see the baby's face better. "But you didn't smell so new a few minutes ago, did you?"

Holly grinned. Mary's statement explained the source of the odor she hadn't been able to locate. She played that thought over in her head and decided that, on a scale of one to ten, with one being the least weird thought she'd ever had and ten being the most weird, a porcelain baby Jesus with a dirty diaper probably got a fifteen.

Mary spoke again, drawing Holly out of her thoughts. "Are you ready for Him?"

If ever Holly had heard a loaded question...

Mary crossed to the empty manger. "He's fed, burped, and changed." A smile curved her lips. "Mothers today have no idea how blessed they are. Disposable diapers? I'd have found a way even on Joseph's limited earnings." She stooped, took a second to untangle little fingers from her hair, and laid the baby down. Her lips brushed his forehead with a kiss before she stood. "I love you, baby boy. He's all yours, Holly." Her gaze met Holly's. "Listen well."

The little mother took her place among the other figurines, and before Holly could exhale, she was quiet and still once again. Holly turned her attention to the baby. Instead of reaching out, she tucked her hands behind her back and held them together tightly. A very adult male voice reached her ears.

"I don't bite."

Holly pressed her lips together, snatched up the baby in the manger—once again a single piece of porcelain—and held it cupped in both hands. Her first sensation was one of a pleasant warmth that started in her fingers, worked its way up her arms, and didn't stop until it enveloped her like a cocoon. With the warmth came something like a prybar that lodged itself in the cracked armor around her heart.

Sage, Riley, Riley's pastor, a set of porcelain figurines, and little Darla. Each one had chipped at that armor until it was pitted and held together by a thread. As Holly held the final piece of the Nativity set, she could almost feel the last piece of her resistance falling away. A feeling Holly didn't recognize filled the void.

Was that love?

"Yes," He said.

Holly looked down at the figure in her hands. Instead of a Baby in a Manger, she saw a grown man sitting on a boulder. His face was bearded, his complexion unmarked, his brown eyes intent and piercing. When their gazes met, Holly simply fell into another place.

In a heartbeat, she found herself sitting on the boulder next to the man. She didn't have to be told who He was. Every cell in her body was screaming His name like they'd been waiting an eternity for His presence.

Jesus smiled at her, His teeth a perfect white crescent in the brown beard. "This will make our talk easier, don't you think?" He took her hand, and Holly felt the warmth gathering a second time. "You know who I am?" Jesus's voice was a rich baritone.

Holly swallowed. Unable to form words, she nodded.

"And you have questions."

"Yes." Holly's voice was an awed whisper.

"Ask away."

Holly waited until she thought she might be able to utter more than a word at a time. "All of this—all of the stories—everything Sage and Riley have been trying to tell me... It's all real?"

"Very real. Your existence on earth is so limited. There is so much going on behind the curtain that you can't see or understand. You may never understand everything, but you must understand this. I love you. My Father loves you."

Holly took the most freeing breath of her life as the words sank in. They burrowed deep under the hurts and neglect of her childhood and awakened hope. "You really came to earth as a baby?"

"Yes."

"And you...died?" The word lingered on Holly's tongue harsh and distasteful. "For me?"

"As it is written."

"Why would You do that?"

Jesus patted her hand. "The psalmist David said that man was made a little lower than the angels, fearfully and wonderfully created. We made man to enjoy fellowship with Us for eternity, and My Father cares for humanity with a love that goes beyond understanding. Each and every one of you are special to Him."

Holly looked into the eyes of Jesus. The sincerity she saw there spoke of a worth she'd never have assigned to herself.

Jesus continued. "When Adam and Eve were deceived in the garden, the Father knew He would need a plan to redeem them and the many who would come after. But the wages of sin is death. Redemption required a sacrifice."

"You." It was a statement, not a question.

"Me. I went willingly. How could I not? Heaven wouldn't be heaven without you there."

"But..." Did Holly dare to ask her questions? Shouldn't she just...just accept what He said? But He'd told her to ask. Gathering her courage, she said, "God knew You would have to die from the beginning, right?"

"We all did."

"Why would You do that?" Holly asked. "Why?"

Jesus kissed her forehead. "Love."

Holly blinked, and the world dissolved a second time. This time, when her vision cleared, she was seated in the garage holding a completely painted baby in a manger. She stared at it, unsure of what had just happened.

"Love, Holly," a voice echoed in her mind. "It was all for love."

CHAPTER TWENTY

She didn't know how long she'd sat at the table, head bowed, tears pooling on the scarred and scratched surface.

"Holly?"

Holly jerked at the sound of her name. She took a moment to pull in a sniffling breath. Through the fog of emotion and revelation, her temples pounded with a headache brought on by the torrent of tears. Her head ached, but for the first time in her life, her heart didn't.

It was free.

"Holly?" Sage spoke again as she crouched at her sister's side. "What's wrong? I thought you came out here to work. You left your phone inside." She held it up. "Riley called."

"You won't believe... Jesus..." No more words would come.

Sage rubbed Holly's arm as she spoke into a phone. "Riley, she can't talk right now. Can you call her back in the morning?"

Holly gathered herself and held out her hand.

"Are you sure?" Sage asked.

"Yes," Holly took the phone with one hand and mopped her face with a paper towel with the other. "What time is it?" she asked before lifting the phone to her ear.

"A little after eight," Sage said. "Have you been out here crying the whole time?"

Holly didn't know how to answer that question. Her time with Jesus had sapped all awareness of time or place. She sent her sister a smile and lifted the phone to her ear.

"Riley, you'll..." Tears flowed again.

"Holly, talk to me. What's wrong?"

"Nothing's wrong, I promise. I've probably never been better in my entire life." Holly swallowed. "Can you come over here? I need to tell you something." She took Sage's hand. "I need to talk to you and Sage both." She looked at the Nativity set. They stared back at her, lifeless and harmless, but she knew better.

She doubted that either of them would believe what she had to say, but she needed to try and make them understand what had happened.

"I can be there in thirty minutes. Are you sure you're OK?"

"I'll let you judge when you get here. Don't break any laws, but hurry, all right?" Holly swiped the call closed after Riley's promise to make the best time he could. She looked up at Sage, who stood with her hands on her hips.

"Out with it," Sage demanded.

Holly stood and pulled her sister into her arms. "I love you." If her feet touched the floor as she crossed to the door, Holly never felt it. The lightness in her spirit had her floating, and every breath she took seemed to fill her deeper than the last. How had she lived twenty-three years so tied up in knots?

It was probably mean to leave Sage hanging until Riley got there, but she supposed Jesus would forgive a little harmless orneriness between siblings. It was Sage's *something spectacular* prayer that had started all of this after all. Holly would thank her later, but for now...

She turned at the door. She had no clue if what she was feeling on the inside was visible on her face, but she didn't know how Sage could fail to see the change. "Riley's on his way. I'm going to go clean up a bit." Her hand shook as she lifted the paper towel to blot her eyes. "My mascara must be all over my face, and I'm sure my hair is a mess."

"Holly, should I be worried about you?"

Holly couldn't help the contented smile that spread across her face. Worried? What was there to worry about? Jesus had brought peace to her life. Why had she pushed against it so desperately?

Thank you, Jesus.

I love you, Holly. I've always loved you.

She felt the words sink down into the freshly turned soil of her heart, and she soaked it up like fertilizer in a flower garden. "It's good, Sage. I promise, it's all good."

By the time Holly finished her story with a whispered, awestruck "Jesus loves me," Sage was weeping in her chair, her face buried in her hands. Riley stood with his fingers tucked in the pockets of his frayed jeans, his gaze moving back and forth between Holly and her worktable where the completed Nativity set rested.

"So you're saying"—Riley's hand swept to indicate the whole set—"these...this..." He cleared his throat, obviously at a loss for adequate words. "My Nativity set talked to you?"

Holly nodded.

Riley stepped closer to the table and crouched down. "Are they talking now?"

Holly picked up the baby and waited for something to happen. "Not a single peep," she said as she replaced the manger on the table. Her heart felt just a smidge empty at the realization. The process had been mind-boggling and scary, but the result had been glorious beyond words. "They had a story to tell. I guess, once that was done, they were done. I don't think I was supposed to tell you guys about it, but since it was sort of your fault, I—"

"*Our* fault?" Sage looked up. "How do you figure?"

Holly put her hands on her hips in mock frustration. "You

prayed for something *spectacular*. Riley offered me money to paint the fool thing."

Riley held up a hand. "You showed this set to me, remember? I didn't even know you at the time. Even if I had"—he waved his upraised hand—"a talking Nativity set is a little out there, even for me."

"Fine," Holly said. "I'll deduct your blame for the Nativity set, but I'm charging you double for the prayers I know you were praying. I'm learning just how effective that tool can be. It's good blame, but blame nevertheless. The way I see it, you two are the ones who are going to have to live with the consequences."

"Consequences?" Riley asked.

"Yep, the way I feel right now, it's a good thing we don't own a ladder. I might just climb up on the roof and tell the neighborhood that Jesus loves them. Your prayers have created a monster."

Riley stepped to her side and draped an arm around her shoulders. "Let's hold off on that. I'm pretty sure we can find more productive things to do with your newfound enthusiasm."

Holly turned into his chest and melted against him. His arms came around her in a full-blown hug. "I've never felt like this in my whole life," she whispered for his ears only. "I know it's late, but would you do me a favor?" When he nodded, she stepped out of his arms.

She glanced at her sister. "Could you give us a minute?"

Sage stood. "Absolutely. I think it's my turn to clean up a bit. She ran a finger under her eye and held the black-stained tip up to the light. "I probably look like a raccoon." She stepped close and studied the figurines on the table. "Thank you." Her voice broke as she followed Holly's example and picked up the baby in the manger. "I don't know if You're still in there, but I know You always hear me. You saved my sister's life."

Holly watched as Sage's lips turned up in a small smile. "Did He say something to you?"

Sage replaced the figurine. "I'll never tell." But she left the room with a bounce to her step that hadn't been there before.

~

When the door closed behind Sage, Riley pulled Holly to him a second time. "I think I could stand here, just like this, for the rest of the night. I'm so proud of you and excited for you." When Holly nestled closer, he bit his lip. This was his dream, but it was sweet torture.

As if reading his mind, Holly stepped out of the embrace. "I've never felt like this before. Is this normal?"

"I guess you need to tell me how you feel before I can answer that."

"This *tell the world about Jesus, give the devil a black eye* feeling. I wasn't totally kidding about the roof."

Riley snagged the chair Sage had vacated, turned it around, and straddled it. He stared up at the woman he was convinced would be a part of his life from here on out. "Completely. Being forgiven is so miraculous, it's hard to keep it to ourselves."

"Exactly." Holly pulled a second chair from under the table and mirrored his pose. "I want you to take me into Ashton before it gets any later."

"What's in Ashton?"

"Cindy and Gilbert. Will you take me to see them? I need to see them. I don't think I can go by myself. I'd ask Sage to go, but there's something..." Holly filled him in on the details of their aborted visit a week before. "There's something going on that I don't understand just yet. I told her what you said about absentee forgiveness. It seemed to help, so thanks for that."

Riley reached across the space and took her hands. "I'm glad you were able to use what I told you to help Sage. But are you really better prepared than she was to face them?"

Holly pressed her lips together and looked away. He could almost see her mind working.

"I think so," she finally said. "When I saw them from a distance, I didn't have the same reaction as Sage. Sage's was white-lipped panic. My reaction was more apathetic, sort of numb. I was like a little kid who convinces herself that there's a monster under the bed, and when they finally get the courage to throw back the blanket, it's just a dust bunny." She stood and circled the table where the Nativity set sat in silent observation.

"What you shared with me was helpful for Sage and seemed to bring her some peace." Holly lifted her hand to her heart. "For me, I think I need to look them in the eye and tell them that they are forgiven. Will you take me?"

Riley stood and dug his keys out of his pocket. It was late but if this was what she needed, he didn't want her making the trip alone. "Let's go."

He followed Holly through the house and stood quietly as she told Sage they'd be back in a little while, but she didn't elaborate on their destination. Riley got her settled in her seat before circling the vehicle and taking his place behind the wheel.

He could tell by the way she fidgeted that she was nervous and not in the mood for conversation. "You want some music?"

"That would be perfect," Holly answered as the car pulled from the curb.

Riley plugged his phone into the dash, and praise music flooded the car. He reached to turn it down. "Sorry, I like loud music when I'm driving by myself."

Holly turned it back up several notches. "I heard this song at your church on Sunday. I like it."

"I can share the playlist if you want."

He watched as she snuggled into her seat, leaned her head back, and closed her eyes. He smiled into the dark when, at the stoplight on the way out of town, Holly reached over and threaded her fingers with his. He didn't know if the contact was motivated by nerves or something more personal, he just knew that the feel of her hand in his felt completely right, and he wanted more. More of her time, more opportunity to see her grow.

They passed under a streetlight, and he cut a quick glance in her direction. Her eyes were still closed but she was awake, her lips moving with the repetitive chorus of the song playing through the speakers. Man, he wanted to feel those lips against his.

I love her, Father. I've tried to help her while protecting my heart, not that it did a lot of good. I've been hooked since the first moment I laid eyes on her. You cleared a path for me tonight. Please look at our futures. If they don't line up together, don't let me invest in something that isn't for me.

The answer was so immediate it took his breath away.

I have ordained you as helpmates for each other.

As the words settled into Riley's consciousness, he raised Holly's hand to his lips and kissed it.

"What was that for?"

Riley kept his eyes on the road so Holly wouldn't see the dopey smile on his face. "Oh, just because."

HOLLY STRAIGHTENED as Riley pulled up to the curb in front of the shabby strip of apartments. It was almost ten p.m. Sort of late for an unannounced visit, but lights shone in the apartment windows. Her gaze roamed the area. There were a couple of streetlights, one at either end of the property, but their stingy glow did little to illuminate the broad space in between. Even without the benefit of adequate light, she could see a landscape of puddles between the car and the apartment. She was going to track mud everywhere when she got back in the car.

Can't be helped.

She reached for the door handle and turned to look at Riley over her shoulder. "You can wait here."

"Not on your life," Riley said. "Sit still for a second." He opened the glove box and pulled out a flashlight. "I'll come around."

Holly waited, glad Riley hadn't agreed to her idea. She wasn't sure what she was going to say to her parents when they opened the door.

She sent up a quick, *Help me.*

I'm with you.

After weeks of being subjected to Gabriel's nearly constant presence in her thoughts, Jesus's answer didn't surprise her nearly as much as it could have. "Thank You," she whispered.

Riley opened the door, held out his hand, and directed the flashlight's beam at the ground. "Watch your step."

They picked their way to the porch. Holly took a deep breath and knocked. The door swung open almost immediately.

"Yeah?"

She took a step back and stared at the tall, heavy, grizzly bear of a man framed in the opening. Surprise stole her words.

Riley stepped forward and held out his hand. "Sorry to bother you so late. "I'm Pastor Soeurs from the food bank. I was here a few days ago, and Cindy Hoffman was ill. I wondered how she was doing."

The big man leaned on the broom he was holding and studied the couple for a few moments. "They ain't here." He reached for the door.

Holly held out a hand to keep the door from closing in their faces. "Do we have the wrong apartment?"

"Look," the man said. "I don't have time for this. I've got to get this place cleaned for new tenants in the morning. If Hoffman owes you money, I'm sorry, but I can't help you. Him and the woman took all their stuff and cleared out of here two days ago. I got no idea where they went. Don't really care. Have a good night."

This time when he closed the door, Holly didn't try to stop him. She stood there, looking at the dirty cement at her feet. Should she laugh or cry? Did it matter either way?

"I'm sorry," Riley whispered.

Her shoulders bobbed. "Nothing to be sorry for. I didn't intend to put myself in a position to be used by them again, but I wanted to let them know that I forgave them."

Riley put his arm around her waist and pulled her close as they walked back to the car. "You can't dictate their actions. Maybe you'll get a chance to talk to them someday, but in the meantime, forgiveness was never about them. God has a plan for your life, and He sees your heart. Obedience is always more important than an outcome we can't control."

There were those words again. *God has a plan for your life.* So everyone said, but she still didn't have a clue. The ride back was quiet as Holly thought about it. She knew she was just at the beginning of something, but she didn't know what that something was or how to find it.

Riley pulled into her drive. "Penny for your thoughts."

"I'm just trying to decide what happens next. As grateful as I am that Jesus saved me, I'm more unsettled now than I was this morning. It's not Gilbert and Cindy. They're just sticking to a lifelong pattern. But..."

"But what?"

Holly shifted in the seat so that she faced him and met his eyes in the dim light of the car. Her heart rate doubled when he smiled at her.

I think you'll like my plan.

This time the words did take Holly by surprise. She swallowed, hardly able to believe what she'd heard. "Everyone's been telling me that God has a plan for my life. Will you help me find it?"

RILEY TOOK both of her hands in his. "Absolutely. I'll help you pray. I'm sure Sage will too. If you listen, He'll direct you." There was so much more in his heart. What would she say if he told her what he was feeling, what God had told him? Could he...should he offer her a hint? Something in his expression must have given his thoughts away.

"There's more to it than that, I think," she whispered.

Riley took a deep breath. *Here goes, God.* "I watched you today while you were at the food bank. I know you didn't want to be there but you're a natural. You were kind and compassionate. Lots of people come to us, and they're embarrassed to be there or afraid of being judged. Something about you puts them at ease. I know you probably don't want to hear this, and I'm not God, but hard as it is for you to believe, maybe part of His plan for you is the food bank. Your experiences make you uniquely qualified."

Holly held his gaze for several seconds, and he watched as a variety of emotions crossed her face.

He pressed his lips together. *Way to push your luck, bud, you need to take a step back.*

To give himself a moment to regroup he opened his door and came around to help her out of the car. Once they started up the walk, he said, "I mean, that's just a thought."

"Would my involvement mean spending more time with the director?"

He bumped her shoulder lightly. "That could be arranged."

They reached the porch and turned to face each other. Riley's whole body tensed when her gaze settled on his mouth. "It wouldn't all have to be work, would it?"

Riley rested his hands on her shoulders. Her eyes, her lips... The soft shadows of the porch were intoxicating. He pulled her close so that their mouths were just a whisper apart. "Holly Hoffman, may I kiss you?"

Her answer was a breathless whisper. "I thought you'd never ask."

Riley pulled Holly into his arms as her eyes fluttered closed. He kissed her eyelids and the tip of her nose. "Look at me." His voice was hoarse and a little breathless. She opened her eyes, and he threaded his fingers in the silky auburn tresses he'd dreamed of touching. "I plan to be a part of whatever God has planned for you."

"Yes, please."

Her words were barely there and sounded more like a prayer than an acknowledgment of his words. His lips met hers in a kiss that held both promise and future.

EPILOGUE

CHRISTMAS EVE

Holly sat amid the clutter and noise of a family Christmas and couldn't remember a time when she'd been happier. Meals with Riley never got old, but when you added his parents and little brother and sister to the mix you got... Well, she wasn't sure what you got, but if whatever it was didn't put a smile on your face, you'd been dead too long for it to matter.

The remnants of a massive feast awaited attention on the dining room table. Probably a chore that should have been completed as soon as the meal was over, but when there were four-year-old twins waiting to open gifts, you did what you had to do.

The area around the Christmas tree looked like a war zone with bits of colorful paper and bright ribbons strewn in every corner and down the hall for good measure. Two shiny new bicycles occupied space near the front door. The twins had been giddy with excitement when Dane's father, dressed in a Santa suit that barely disguised his identity, wheeled them through the front door with a loud "Ho ho ho!" The bikes were just one gift among dozens for the exuberant youngsters.

The twins weren't the only ones with gifts to open. Mac had bought Dane a new table saw, and he'd produced tickets for a family vacation to Disney World after the new year. Holly could not hold back the tears when he'd hastened to tell her that there was a ticket for her if she wanted to come along. Holly'd blubbered a "yes" as she'd hugged Riley's father. They'd made her part of their family over the last couple of months. Holly was surprised almost every day at the joy those new relationships gave her.

Her relationship with Christ was another thing that brought Holly joy. Every day seemed to hold some new tidbit of growth or wisdom or peace.

And then there was Riley. She watched from under her lashes as he opened a gift from the twins. She wasn't quite sure what her future with him held, but for now, being in love with the hottest guy in Garfield was enough. She'd juggled her schedule and managed to spend two afternoons a week at the food bank. She was still amazed at the satisfaction that brought her.

"Do you like it?"

Zachary's question jolted Holly back to the present as Riley took a bright red knitted scarf out of the box. Holly grinned as he unfolded it. It had to be at least ten feet long.

"Well, do you?" Aimee asked. "We picked it out special from the Santa store at school."

Riley looked from the scarf, to his siblings, to his mother. His eyebrows were hiked when he said, "Santa has his own store?"

Mac laughed. "Sort of a flea market the preschool teachers set up. The kids get to bring five dollars to school and go shopping."

"Ah." Riley stood and wrapped the scarf around his neck. "I love it. Thanks, guys."

"You're welcome," Zach said.

Aimee held a slightly squished box in Holly's direction. "We shopped for you too."

Holly pulled the little girl into a hug. "You're the best. Thanks." She unwrapped the gift and pulled out a scarf of her own. This one was purple and ruffled, but at least it didn't hang to the floor. She put it around her neck. "Thanks, you two. It's perfect."

Riley headed for the garage. "I've got to go get a special gift. I'll be right back."

He was going for the Nativity set, and Holly was suddenly on pins and needles to see if Mac's reaction was worth the time and money the gift represented. To distract herself, she turned her thoughts to her friends and what she imagined them doing tonight.

Ruthies two daughters had surprised her with tickets for a ten-day cruise. They were enjoying a Caribbean vacation for the holidays. Holly could just see the three of them walking along a white, sandy beach while the people at home dealt with the snow in tomorrow's forecast. She looked at her watch. By now Maggie would be rushing to spend Christmas Eve with her kids and the foster father who had become more and more a part of her life over the last few months. If God was faithful, and He always was, those kids would be coming home with Maggie for good sooner rather than later.

Ember had surprised everyone last week with her announcement that she and Quinn would welcome a new baby in the summer. Quinn was over the moon, and the girls were ecstatic. They were all hoping for a boy and were counting the days until an ultrasound revealed the substance of this very special gift.

But not everyone was having a joyous Christmas. Piper had given birth to a stillborn baby back in October. The group of friends were still reeling from that. God was always good, but sometimes there were no good answers to the hard questions. For Lacy, the holidays had thrown her into a period of renewed mourning for her daughter, Olivia. Holly didn't know who she felt sorrier for. Lacy or Lacy's husband, Cole, who'd been behind the wheel when the accident happened.

And finally, there was Sage. Her sister had turned down the invitation to join this gathering to attend a Christmas function at her church. Holly couldn't be one hundred percent sure, but she thought there might be a guy involved in her sister's decision. The thought made her smile. If Sage could find the sort of happiness Holly'd found, then life would be just about perfect.

Jesus, watch over each of them tonight. Give them the peace and the joy You've given me. Help each of them find Your path for their lives in the months ahead.

Riley came back carrying the huge box he and Holly had wrapped together.

"Oh, my goodness," Mac exclaimed. "Who's the lucky person?"

"That would be you." Riley set the box on the floor in front of his mother's chair. "It's breakable, so don't go crazy." He took his place back on the sofa with Holly. Holly clasped his hand and added to her prayer. *Please let her like it.*

She held her breath as Mac opened the big box and extracted the smaller boxes one by one. The first box held the wooden crèche that Riley had constructed to house the Nativity set.

Mac smiled as she turned it this way and that. She looked at Riley. "It's lovely. Did you make it?"

"Yep." Riley made a motion with his finger. "Keep going."

Mac raised her eyebrows and picked up the next box. No one spoke as the figurines were unwrapped, examined, and set to the side. When the whole set was exposed, Mac stood and crossed to where Riley was sitting. She pulled him to his feet. "I don't think I've ever seen anything so beautiful or more perfect. Thank you."

Riley hugged her back. "They had your name on them the moment I saw them. I'm so glad you like it."

Mac released him. "I don't like it, I love it." She turned to Holly. "And I don't have to be told who painted them. I've never seen anyone as talented as you."

Holly blushed under the praise and glanced at the figurines. "It was a...special experience."

The understatement of the century.

The blush and praise made Holly uncomfortable. She scrambled to her feet. "That looks like all the gifts. Let me help you clear the table. I saw a chocolate cake in the kitchen that I can't wait to try."

From behind her, Riley cleared his throat. "Not so fast. There's one more gift."

When Holly turned, she found Riley on one knee next to the sofa. He held his heart in his eyes and a tiny box in his hands. Her mouth went dry, and her knees went weak as she sank back to the sofa cushion.

Riley opened the box to reveal a sparkling ring.

A flash of light had Holly blinking. She looked for the source and found Mac in the corner with a camera. She put it away and motioned to her husband. "Dane, grab the twins. It's time for dessert in the kitchen."

"I want pie," Aimee said as she ran from the room.

"Ice cream!" Zachary yelled as he followed.

Once they were alone, Riley took Holly's hand. "Holly Elizabeth Hoffman, I fell in love with you the moment I laid eyes on you. You brighten every day we spend together, and I want to spend every day I have left loving you. Will you marry me?"

Holly closed her eyes and tried to breathe past the lump in her throat. She just needed air for one word. She found more than that. "Yes. Yes for today, yes for tomorrow." Her voice broke, and she gave in to the happiest tears of her life. "Yes for forever."

Riley took the ring from the box and slipped it on her finger. He pulled her to her feet and into his arms. "I love you so much."

He lowered his head and sealed his words with a kiss so tender that Holly thought she might melt into a puddle at his feet. Riley ended the kiss but held her in a firm hug for several seconds. Over his shoulder, Holly caught sight of the Nativity set. She blinked.

For just a second, she thought the angel winked at her.

She can't escape the mistakes of her past...
Callie Stillman has done everything she can to bury the memories of a tiny, baby-sized coffin. She lives life one day at a time, basking in the love of a good man and doting on her grandchildren. Until she crosses paths with a little girl who is obviously in trouble—but tries to hide it.

They can't trust anyone...
Iris and Samantha Evans are living on borrowed time. Deserted, orphaned, betrayed, and deceived, they need rescuing in the worst way.

He's praying for a miracle...
Steve Evans had his life changed by God. A reformed drug addict, he's searching for the family he abandoned ten years ago...

When Callie can no longer ignore the signs that Iris needs help, her interference sends four people on a collision course that will force her to face the past she'd rather forget.

ALSO BY SHARON SROCK

THE COMPLETE *LADIES OF GARFIELD* SERIES

CALLIE

TERRI

PAM

SAMANTHA

KATE

KARLA

HANNAH'S ANGEL

A MAKEOVER MADE IN HEAVEN

IRIS

MAC

RANDY

CHARLEY

JESSE

SYD

ALEX

***

THE MERCIE SERIES

FOR MERCIE'S SAKE

BEGGING FOR MERCIE

ALL ABOUT MERCIE

THE MERCIE COLLECTION

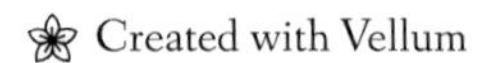
Created with Vellum

Made in the USA
Monee, IL
11 October 2021